ONE AGAINST EIGHT

Slade crouched in the narrow rock crevice, waiting—his back against rock and a shoulder touching each wall. Directly in front of him was the opening in the crevice —the only way out.

Outside, eight killers closed in. Slade could hear them but he could not see them. The waiting slashed at his nerves.

A shadow fell across the opening. Slade fired and a man fell prone across the aperture. One against seven.

Another shadow moved, only this time it was a boulder, coming at Slade. Another came and another, missing him by inches.

He straightened, a gun in each hand. Better to die fighting than to be squashed like a bug. Tense as a coiled spring, Slade moved toward the opening—his guns ready to meet death with death!

AMBUSH TRAIL

by Bradford Scott

WILDSIDE PRESS

ONE

"SHADOW, IT SMELLS like somebody is cooking somewhere up that crack in the hills."

Ranger Walt Slade, whom the peons of the Mexican river villages named El Halcon—The Hawk—sniffed with appreciation the aroma drifting down the narrow brush-grown valley, more enticing to a hungry man than the perfume of roses, the fragrance of frying meat and steaming coffee.

"And seeing as the provision poke is empty and I can't subsist on vegetation like you can, you old grass burner, we'll just mosey up there and see if there's a chance to share pot luck with those gents, whoever they are," he continued to his tall black horse. Shadow snorted what was apparently acquiescence to the proposal and Slade sent him pacing forward through the red blaze of the low lying afternoon sun.

Slade's saddle pouches were devoid of anything to eat, the last scrap having been washed down with brook water some twenty hours before, most of which hours had been spent in the saddle. So it was not unnatural that El Halcon craved a substantial "surrounding," rangeland parlance for a square meal.

Slade rode at a fair pace but did not push his horse over the rough ground, for the trail he followed up the valley was really nothing but a game track fringed on each side by brush. He had covered something better than a mile when to his ears came the sound of voices, and he slowed Shadow a trifle. This was wild land between the Quitman Mountains and the Finlay Range, with the verdant Middle Valley of the Rio Grande to the west. Of late the section had been plagued by an outlaw bunch that appeared to be working steadily westward, which was why Walt Slade was in the vicinity.

Slowing his mount still more, Slade tried to catch snatches of the conversation going on beyond the screen of tall brush. He was somewhat reassured by the cheerful timbre of the voices and the frequent laughter. Neither was of the nature of talk usually indulged in by men who know that a peace officer and his posse might well be on their trail. There was no attempt to keep the voices down and they sounded carefree.

Still, Slade took no chances. He could be mistaken in his estimate of whoever was camped ahead. Shadow was proceeding at a slow walk with the split reins looped and hanging on his neck, and Slade's hands were close to the black butts of the heavy guns protruding from their carefully worked and oiled cut-out holsters when the growth thinned and the camp came into view.

Grouped around a fire were seven men in cowhand garb, their shirts and overalls and boots splashed with mud and dust. They were fresh-faced young fellows with one grizzled exception. Slade pulled up and waved his hand.

The group around the fire saw a tall man, broad of shoulder and deep of chest, with a lean, deeply-bronzed face dominated by long black-lashed eyes of pale gray. Cold, reckless eyes that nevertheless had little devils of laughter dancing in their clear depths. He had a rather wide mouth, grin-quirked at the corners, that relieved somewhat the sternness, almost fierceness, evinced by the prominent high-bridged nose above and the powerful jaw and chin beneath. He wore the homely garb of the rangeland in a manner that lent distinction to faded levis, soft blue shirt and well scuffed half-boots. A vivid handkerchief was looped about his throat, double cartridge belts encircled his sinewy waist and his pushed-back "J.B." revealed thick hair so black a blue shadow seemed to lie upon it. He sat his magnificent black horse with the easy grace of a lifetime in the saddle.

The men about the fire were evidently satisfied with what they saw, for they shouted a greeting.

"Light off, feller, and feed your tapeworm," one called. "Just getting ready to sit down. Got a helpin' of oats for the cayuse— Blazes! but he's a beauty!"

Hungry enough to chew cactus spines, Slade was not slow in accepting the invitation. He got the rig off Shadow

so the big horse could feed and roll in comfort and without delay went to work on the loaded plate and steaming
cup handed him.

"Eat hearty, feller, we got plenty of chuck," said the
one oldster of the group. "Laid in a good supply before
we moseyed into this crack."

"Funny place for a bunch of waddies to be squatting,"
Slade commented smilingly.

"Uh-huh," said the other, while his companions chuckled. "But you see, feller, we're on the run from the Law."

The others ducked their heads in sober agreement.

Somehow, Slade was not particularly impressed by this
frank confession of wrong-doing.

"How come?" he asked.

"It's a short story but a sad one," the oldtimer sighed.
"Us fellers all work for the Cross-in-a-Box, a good spread.
Or did. Over to Vanton we had a little disagreement with
some poker-playing gents after we caught a tinhorn cold-
decking the game. Nobody got hurt much, but before the
arg'fyin' was finished, nearly every table and chair in the
joint was busted, the bar was turned over and the back-
bar lookin' glass shot to hash. As it happens, the sheriff
owns a half-interest in the place and we knew he'd be a
mite wrathy. Fact is, we got word he was coming after us
and figured to throw us in the calaboose and keep us there
till we tripped over our whiskers. That didn't sound so
good."

"I can appreciate your feelings in the matter," Slade
smiled. The oldster nodded gravely.

"So," he said, "we figured it would be a good notion
to trail our twine and hole up a while till the sheriff got
over his peeve. We stuffed our pouches with chuck and
headed west. We come to this crack in the hills and it
looked favorable. So we slid into it. That was six weeks ago
and we've been here ever since, except for one or two of
us sneaking out for a fresh supply of eatin' matter now and
then."

"You mean to say the sheriff is still on the prod against
you?" Slade asked in surprise.

"Oh, guess he's got over his mad spell," the oldtimer
replied. "Not that it matters over much; we can buy him a
whole new saloon if we take a notion."

'And that old coot is to blame for everything," another

puncher broke in. "We were poor and happy when we landed here, and if it wasn't for his loco notions we'd still be poor and happy. Because of him we're rich and got responsibilities and may have to turn plumb respectable."

"And now what in blazes are you talking about?" Slade asked wonderingly.

"It's like this," said the cowboy. "That old coot, while he was out of jail for a while, did some placer mining over in California."

"A heck of a lot of it," the old waddie interjected. "Before I went loco and took to following a cow's tail."

"So he says," said the other. "Well, he moseyed around in this valley and got real excited. Swore it was perfect placer-mining country and that we'd oughta try our hand at a bit of digging. We weren't over-interested, but he kept yammering about it until we agreed to give it a whirl, just to shut him up."

"Well?" Slade remarked.

"Darned if the old hellion wasn't right," said the cowboy. "The valley is a real placer section and we've dug up a hefty passel of nuggets and dust—in those pokes over there."

Slade glanced at the stack of plump sacks and nodded thoughtfully. The cowboy shot a meaningful look at his companions, who nodded their heads. He turned back to Slade.

"Feller, you look to be a right sort," he said, "so we're invitin' you to stick around a spell and do a little digging on your own account. Won't take you but a couple of weeks to root out more'n you could tie onto at 'forty-per' in a month of Sundays. What do you say?"

"Gracias," Slade replied. "A heap of thanks, but I've got to be on my way in the morning."

He little thought he was destined to spend quite a few days in the valley.

"Well, if you can't, you can't," the oldtimer said cheerfully, "but you're plumb welcome."

Night had fallen as they sat eating and talking. Overhead the stars blazed golden in a sky of blue velvet. The night was very still, the silence broken only by the purl and ripple of the little stream that flowed nearby. The cowboys lounged around the fire, joking and chaffing one another, anticipating the high times they would enjoy when they should go back to town and convert their gold into money that would itch to be spent.

A thick chaparral growth hemmed the camp on three sides, and under the spreading branches the shadows were black as the mouth of a cave. Shadow, grazing nearby, suddenly lifted his head and blew softly through his nose. Slade, sensitive to all the moods of his horse, was starting to rise when from the black "cave mouth" spurted lances of flame. The hills rocked to a roar of gunfire.

Four of the seven punchers went down at that first murderous volley. The others jerked their guns and fought back at the hidden drygulchers.

Walt Slade, shot through the body and creased along the forehead, staggered to his feet, a blazing gun in each hand. Lurching drunkenly, he reeled back out of the circle of firelight as a deep and powerful voice rang out, "Let them have it!" and the hidden guns boomed again. Lead whistled all about him as he fell. By a superhuman effort he got to his feet again but he was well nigh unconscious, blinded by the blood that streamed into his eyes. Still gripping his empty guns, he tried to pull the triggers once more. He was utterly confused, his sense of direction lost. He tried to run to the aid of the stricken punchers but, bewildered, his head whirling dizzily, he staggered away from the campfire instead of toward it. A score of faltering steps, a scrambling, lurching fall and he was dimly conscious of rending bushes, of twigs whipping his face, of a terrific shock. He made a last spasmodic effort, rolled over and over. Then blackness closed in on him, fold on clammy fold, and for him all was silence and peace.

TWO

IT WAS DAYLIGHT when Slade recovered consciousness. He was sick, weak, for he had lost a great deal of blood. There was a hot throb in his left side; his head ached abominably. For some time he lay in a haze of discomfort, dazedly trying to figure just what had happened. Gathering a little strength, he managed to examine his wounds.

The bullet scrape along his forehead was of little consequence, but the wound in his side was a different matter. Although it was bad enough, he was thankful to learn by various symptoms that while the bullet had gone clean through a few inches below the heart, it was well to the left and hadn't injured any vital organs. Exhausted by his efforts, he relaxed for another period. Then he began to wonder how he happened to be alive at all and made shift to inspect his surroundings.

He found he was lying in a deep hollow that had been cut under the creek bank by high water. Brush and creepers grew down over the bank and hung across the hole into which he had tumbled, so that in the darkness nothing could be seen of the hollow from the outside. To which he knew he owed his almost miraculous preservation. Had the drygulchers discovered him when they searched for him, as he figured they must have, he would certainly not have been numbered among the living.

Painfully, slowly he crawled out of the hole and up the bank. His side burned like fire and a bubbly mist floated before his eyes. Finally he made it to the crest and peered cautiously through a final fringe of growth.

The site was quiet and peaceful, with the peace and quiet of death. The horses grazed in the little clearing, all except Shadow, who stood with ears pricked, staring toward the brush behind which Slade crouched. Slade watched him for a moment or two, but the horse did not

10

turn his head, and did not blow through his nose. Also, he remained out in the open, which he would not have done if somebody were holed up in the growth nearby.

"Gone, all right," Slade muttered. "Guess it's safe to get from under cover." He eased through the brush, walking slowly, his body rigid. The camp was a scene of horror.

All seven of the cowboys were dead, tumbled this way and that. A glance told him that the sacked gold was gone. However, the rigs had not been bothered, nor the plenitude of provisions, so far as he could see. Moving carefully so as not to start his wounds bleeding afresh, he drew a roll of bandage and a pot of antiseptic ointment from his own untouched saddle pouches. He worked off his shirt and proceeded to pad and strap his injured side. This done, he sat down beside the ashes of the dead fire, very weak and again feeling sick. He got the fire going and heated some left-over coffee which he drank as hot as he could swallow it. Although he did not feel much like eating, he cooked a meal and ate slowly, downing as much as he could. Then with fingers that trembled woefully, he rolled a cigarette.

While he smoked, he contemplated the bodies strewn about and decided he could do nothing for them at the moment; but he did manage to drag some of the food off a ways and make a new camp. Then he stretched out on a blanket in the shade of an overhang and was almost instantly asleep.

The next thing Slade knew, it was getting dark. His side was painfully sore and he was still very weak, but his iron constitution was throwing off the effects of his injuries and his strength was returning. He cooked and ate again, and again went to sleep. He awoke with the dawn feeling much better. The two openings of the wound were already closing and in that clean, dry air he had little fear of complications.

He felt so much better that, after cooking and eating his breakfast, he resolved to bury the bodies of the slain cowboys. Working slowly, with frequent rest periods, he dug a wide and shallow grave in which he placed the bodies. Finished, he stood for a moment gazing across the low mound that would be brown and bare until the new grass was grown. His face was bleak, his eyes cold.

El Halcon was not given to dramatics; he merely bowed his black head a moment, then turned away. But those who knew him would not have traded places with that outlaw bunch for all the gold the valley might produce.

Slade remained in the valley for three more days, until his strength was fully recovered and there was no longer any serious danger of breaking open the wounds. Getting the rig on Shadow, now fully fed and rested, he rode from the valley and turned the big black's nose west, the direction he was confident the owlhoot band had taken. He settled himself in the saddle, spoke to Shadow and the horse quickened his pace. Slade's eyes swept the far distant horizon that kept receding in time with the beat of Shadow's hoofs. El Halcon was riding the vengeance trail.

Slade knew there was a railroad way station only a few miles ahead, and that a telegraph operator would be on duty there. Reaching the station, he dismounted and entered the shack. From a concealed secret pocket in his broad leather belt he slipped out something and laid it on the operator's table. It was a gleaming silver star set on a silver circle, the feared and honored badge of the Texas Rangers.

The operator glanced at the star and ducked his head respectfully.

"What can I do for you, Ranger?" he asked.

Slade wrote out a terse message and handed it to the operator. It was addressed to Captain Jim McNelty, the famed Commander of the Border Batallion, and read:

It happened in Texas. I'm riding west.

"Should be an answer in an hour or so, if Captain Jim is at Post Headquarters, as he is likely to be," Slade told the operator. "I'll wait."

In less than an hour the answer came, which caused the operator to stare and Slade to chuckle:

Ride to the Pacific Ocean if necessary, blast you.
Then bridge it and keep going.

Still chuckling, Slade left the station. He knew the cryptic message meant that he had Captain Jim's approval of whatever he might do and all the time he might require in which to do it. Next thing was to pick up the trail of the outlaws, the same band, he was convinced, that he had been trailing from east of Van Horn.

The first day of easy riding brought no results. But the evening of the second he learned what confirmed his belief that the bunch was heading west, very likely into the mountain country of New Mexico, unless they decided to circle about and re-enter the wilder fastnesses of the Texas Big Bend. Slade was of the opinion, however, that the outlaws were leaving Texas, which was the reason for his sending the telegram to Captain McNelty.

Already into the Middle Valley of the Rio Grande, with sunset not far off, Slade paused at the house of a gent who combined ranching with grape growing, the section having for years been famous for its grapes and the golden wine made from them. A hospitable invitation to cool his saddle and spend the night was accepted gratefully and, after the evening meal, Slade drew the owner into conversation, adroity steering the talk into certain channels.

"Yep, we get visitors every now and then," the rancher replied to an indirect question. "Most of 'em are okay, but once in a while some show up we could do without, although nobody has ever made us any trouble. About a week ago, a bunch stopped here that sort of gave me the creeps, though they were civil enough. Salty looking jiggers, for fair. One carried his arm in a sling. Said a steer's horn punched a hole in it. Maybe, but I figure that 'horn' had a lead tip with gunpowder back of it. Another one limped bad. He said his horse pitched him, but I noticed there were a couple of holes in the leg of his overalls that sure weren't made by cigarette ashes. They'd been in a ruckus, all right, no doubt about it."

"Where were they headed?" Slade asked casually.

"West, I gathered," the rancher replied. "They asked some questions about El Paso, but I don't think they aimed to stop there. Heading for New Mexico, I'd say."

After Slade said good-bye to the friendly rancher the following morning and rode off, his host watched him out of sight, then turned and spoke to his range boss.

"I noticed he had what looked mighty like a bullet burn on the front of his head, and there were a couple of holes in his shirt, too. Shirt had been washed recent, but there were some stains that didn't plumb wash out, and it seemed to me he sort of favored his left side. Uh-huh, not much doubt but it was him that bunch had the run-in with. And I figure they'd be doing themselves a big favor to ride mighty fast and mighty far. A nice feller, but I sure wouldn't want to have that big ice-eyed hellion on my trail!"

THREE

THE TRAIL RUNNING WEST to El Paso traversed a terrain of wild and desolate grandeur. Rugged mountains towered skyward, their rocky crests shouldering away the clouds, their mighty shoulders grown with gray-green chaparral that toward evening was swathed in purple shadow. From their bases salt flats extended for miles without end. Pines and oaks dotted the high areas, while the lower levels were a tangle of sage-brush, cacti and bear grass. During the sunlight hours, weird, heat-created mirages appeared with startling suddenness and clarity, to disappear just as abruptly and be replaced by others, shifting, changing, bewildering the traveller, filling the superstitious with quaking fears. The heat devils danced and dust-laden balls of weed whirled across the trail to beat themselves to pieces against the rocks, seeming to writhe in agony as they simulated the flagellants of old. And through their dry death rattle knifed the sinister buzz of the rattlesnake and the echoing plaint of the hunting wolf.

A desert of salt-impregnated sand gleamed ghastly white in the moonlight and blindingly glaring under the sun. In the far distance the deathly white was broken by vivid blue-green splashes of color, made by shallow lakes, their brackish waters ringed with low dunes of almost pure salt. Salt for which wars were fought and blood was shed from Indian times to later years. The heat shimmering and weaving gave those lakes the eerie, unreal appearance of floating low in the superheated atmosphere, their brilliantly colored waters seeming to flicker in flame-like animation.

A wild and savage land in which savage deeds were done, even on the edge of the broad and fertile valley which replaced salt desert and sandy hills.

Between the rocky heights of the Sierra Tinaja Pintas

15

and the Sierra Diablos crouched the cattle and mining town of Hueco, little more than a straggling village but prosperous because of being a supply depot for ranches and mines.

Hills, bleak, inhospitable, edged close to Hueco, throwing their frowning shadows across the town in the early morning and late evening hours. From the hills writhed furtive trails to join with the broad track rolling on to El Paso.

Hueco boasted, among other things, a bank. It was a solid, substantial bank and there was usually a very large sum of money in its big old vault—mine, ranch and fruit grower payroll and supply money as well as deposits, for the Hueco bank serviced many miles of productive territory.

The contents of that vault must have been tempting to gentlemen of easy conscience who often rode that way; but the bank official and employees were able and alert men hired as much for their proficiency with the six-shooter as for their nimbleness at figures. Moreover they looked with suspicion on all strangers until they had satisfactorily proven themselves.

However there was certainly nothing suspicious about the two prospectors trudging along the narrow track which writhed down from the brush covered hills to the north and joined the main trail less than a hundred feet from the east wall of the bank building.

They were typical bewhiskered desert rats, their hair unkempt, their faded shirts and overalls a network of patches, their hats floppy, their boots scuffed and run-over at the heels. Driving two laden burrows ahead of them, they turned into the main trail, which was Hueco's main street.

In front of the bank they paused, staring at its legended windows, speaking together, nodding their heads as in agreement. From the burros' packsacks they took two big rawhide pokes, well plumped out, that appeared surprisingly heavy for their size. Side by side they entered the bank, gazed around a moment, then approached the cashier's brass-grilled window.

The cashier watched them closely, for he took no chances even with harmless looking prospectors.

"Something I can do for you, gentlemen?" he asked, one hand beneath the counter.

"Yep, maybe you can," replied the foremost prospector. "Do you fellers buy gold?"

"We arrange with the Government assay offices to have it bought," the cashier explained. "We weigh any we receive and give a receipt for the number of ounces."

The prospector nodded. "And maybe you'd advance a couple of fellers a few pesos on it so they can spend a little time in town?"

"Why, yes, that can usually be arranged," the cashier answered. "Do you have some?"

For answer the prospector heaved one of the rawhide sacks onto the counter shelf with a solid thump. He fumbled the pucker string, up-ended the sack and poured forth before the astounded banker's eyes a flood of nuggets from raisin size to that of a small potato, some of which rolled under the grating onto the cashier's side of the counter.

"For the love of Pete!" gasped the official. The prospector chuckled creakily.

"Here's another poke the same size," he said, thumping the second sack onto the counter. "Yep, we struck it sorta rich."

"And that's putting it mildly!" said the cashier. "Where in blazes did you get it?"

The prospector jerked a thumb to the north. "Up there in the hills," he said. "Plenty more where this come from. We staked out claims, but there's lots more good ground. We figure to spend a few days in town—have us a little bust. When we go back anybody who wants to is plumb welcome to come along and help themselves to ground; we ain't no hogs and the claims we staked, all legal like, will pan us all we want."

The cashier called to his fellow workers, who were craning their necks for a peek:

"Come here, boys, and see what these fellows brought in! Just come and take a look!"

There is something about raw gold that sends fire pulsing through the veins. Men accustomed to counting stacks of double eagles without emotion feel their hearts pound, their breath come short at sight of a heap of the dully yellow treasure plucked from its bed of ages in the earth. The bank employees crowded about the cashier, fingering the nuggets, hefting them, exclaiming. So absorbed were they that they did not hear the seven horsemen ride down the track from the hills, leading two spare mounts. In front of the bank they dismounted and leaving one man to hold the horses, rushed into the building.

The cashier, hearing a sound at the door, glanced up—and looked into the muzzles of two levelled guns!

"Elevate!" blared the "prospector." "Get 'em up! We don't want to kill anybody, but we will if we have to. Get 'em up!"

The bankers "got 'em up." There was nothing else to do. It seemed to them the room was filled with gun muzzles, all pointing in their direction. Seething with anger, they stood rigid, hands high in the air.

The robbers worked with the precision of a well oiled machine. One, tall and broad-shouldered and black-haired, his hatbrim pulled low over his eyes, his neckerchief muffled up around his mouth, scrambled cat-like over the metal grill, unlocked the door and flung it open. Two more instantly joined him. The "prospector," grinning, thriftily scooped up the nuggets and restored them to the rawhide pouch.

The three men inside the inner room, each bearing a large canvas sack, entered the vault, the door of which stood open, and swiftly cleaned it of everything they considered worth taking, and it was plenty. With their companions covering the bankers they whisked out of the building to the waiting horses. The others backed out, guns ready for instant action. Last of all was the pseudo-prospector.

"So long, gents, much obliged for the advance," he said.

The cashier, white with rage, made the mistake of lowering his hands and reaching under the counter for a gun. He paid for the mistake with a bullet hole between his eyes.

Instantly a roar of gunfire from the street blasted the windows to fragments. The bank employees hit the floor, and stayed there till they heard the thud of hoofs receding on the trail. By the time they got to the door, the outlaws had whisked onto the track that ran into the hills and vanished from sight.

FOUR

It was but a few hours after the robbery that Walt Slade rode into Hueco. Very quickly he divined that something was or had been taking place. Knots of men stood on street corners and before saloons, gesticulating, speaking together in excited tones. He noted that as he passed the groups, they fell silent and gazed at him suspiciously. He pulled up beside one.

"Livery stable?" he asked.

"Right around the next corner," a man replied, gesturing with his thumb. The others gazed without speaking.

"Thanks," Slade acknowledged, and rode on.

The stable keeper gave him a keen and appraising glance, and was apparently satisfied with what he saw.

"Feller who rides a horse like this one must be okay," he remarked inconsequentially. "I'll take good care of him." He shot Slade another speculative glance.

"Trough in back, soap and towels, if you'd like to wash up," he offered.

"That will be fine," Slade replied. He asked no questions and showed no concern at the keeper's attitude of hesitancy; this was not the place to get information. He knew just where to go for that.

"Place to eat?" the keeper replied to the question he did ask. "The Aces-Up right across the street from the corner puts out good chuck; drinks about average."

Slade thanked him again and headed for the Aces-Up, which he located without difficulty.

The Aces-Up proved to be a typical cow country saloon. There was a long bar spanning one side of the room, a lunch counter, tables for leisurely eaters, two roulette wheels, a faro bank, tables for gaming, and a dance floor, now unoccupied.

All this he took in at one swift glance as he walked to the bar and ordered a drink. A hush fell over the fairly crowded room when he entered and he knew he was the cynosure of all eyes; evidently all strangers were suspect at the moment.

Toying with his glass, he studied the bartender, who appeared to be a jovial individual and less affected by whatever had happened than were the patrons. He concluded that with him direct methods would be best.

"What's going on?" he asked. "Folks 'pear to be all worked up about something."

"You're darn right they're worked up, cowboy," the drink juggler returned. "No wonder they are. First time anything like it ever happened to this pueblo. Wait a minute till I take care of those gents down the bar and I'll tell you about it."

He hurried away to attend to the wants of impatient customers, then came back to Slade, poured himself a drink and downed it at a gulp. He wiped his handle-bar mustache with great care, twirled it into position, eyed the result in the back bar with satisfaction and turned and nodded.

"Here's how it was," he said, and proceeded to regale the Ranger with an account, in meticulous detail, of what had happened.

"And the hellions sure worked it slick." he concluded. "Slick and fast. Nobody had any notion of what was going on until the shooting started. And by the time folks got their heads out the door the horned toads were on their way. Killed poor Carroway, the cashier, and cleaned the vault of better'n sixty thousand. They went up that snake track of a trail just the other side of the bank. That trail runs straight through the hills to the New Mexico mountains; that's where they're headed for, all right. The boys got a posse together in a hurry and lit out after them. Figure they've got a good chance to catch them up before they cross the state line. They won't stop there, though; they'll follow the sidewinders clean to Colorado if necessary. Yep, they figure to catch 'em up."

Slade nodded, but he did not think the boys would; he had not altered his opinion that the bunch was headed west and would keep on going while the posse wasted their time and energy in the north. Being thoroughly familiar with similar hill trails, originally beaten out by Indian bands raiding across the valley into Mexico, he had a very good idea as to what was to be found higher in the hills, and quite likely the outlaws also knew just what to look for. He finished his drink, sat down at a table and ordered a meal.

Slate ate in a leisurely fashion, but with the appetite of a man who has known what it is to find good food scarce. He ordered a final cup of coffee, rolled and lighted a cigarette and gave himself over to reflection.

There was no doubt in his mind but that the bank robbers were the bunch he was trailing. The gold the "prospector" displayed was very likely part of the loot stolen from the cowboys murdered in the valley to the east. El Halcon's face grew grim, his eyes even colder than usual as he thought of that pitiless slaughter. He dismissed the incident as a deterrent to clear thinking and concentrated on the more recent happening. A slick bunch, all right, and utterly snake-blooded. And a man at the head with brains and the ability to use them. Slade lounged back comfortably in his chair and pondered the situation in detail.

Gradually a plan took form in his mind. A plan that would be fraught with serious danger to himself but which, he believed, might work even against heavy odds. It all depended on what was farther up in the rugged hills, but he felt pretty sure he'd find there just what he expected.

A discussion of the robbery was going full blast again and men no longer lowered their voices. He listened for some time, hoping to glean further information but without avail. Evidently the barkeep had put out all there was to learn. He glanced through the window at the sun, which was slanting west, and decided it was time to be moving. Saying goodbye to the friendly bartender, he headed for the stable, where he found Shadow fed and refreshed.

"Be seeing you sometime," he told the keeper. "Stop here if I happen along this way again."

The keeper watched him ride away, his face thoughtful. "Now just what is *he?*" he asked an unresponsive feed box. "Looks to be a chuck line riding cowhand, but somehow I got a feeling he ain't. Blazes! What a pair of eyes!

Go through you like a greased knife. I've a notion they don't miss much, and somehow I can't help thinking he's on somebody's trail. Darn glad I ain't that somebody."

The keeper had never met the fruit grower farther east, at whose hospitable casa Slade spent a night, but their conclusions anent El Halcon were singularly in accord.

Glances followed Slade as he rode out of town and he knew he was the subject of conjecture; but to that he paid no mind. Hueco and its inhabitants and what they thought were no longer of any interest to him. His attention was fixed on the brush covered slopes of the hills on his right, slopes that ran upward to a rounded skyline with the bristles of thicket catching the light of the western sun on their thorny tips and the withered leaves turned to flakes of dead gold the brighter for the shadows beneath.

He rode steadily but slowly, for what he sought would quite likely be but a narrow rift in the encroaching chaparral, easy to miss.

Finally he spotted it, a faint trail winding upward. Another of the tracks beaten hard by untold numbers of moccasined feet padding south throughout the centuries, purposeful feet with purposeful and not kindly intent on the lush valley and the inhabited south bank of the Rio Grande.

Without hesitation he turned Shadow's head north and began the winding ascent.

The old trail was tortuous, with the thorny brush crowding close on either side, but the hard packed earth supported very little growth and Shadow had no difficulty negotiating it. He gave an occasional snort of anger when a thorn raked his haunch and glanced back at his rider as if to say, "You can pick the darndest messes to get into!" But for the most part he progressed in steady silence.

As was his habit, Slade was alert and watchful, although he did not expect any obstacles other than those provided by nature on the trip up the slope. Later it would be different, if his conclusions were correct, and he believed they were. He eyed every bend, attuned his ears to all sounds, watched birds that darted to and fro across the track, and analyzed noises made by little animals in the brush. Through rifts in the thickets he checked the westering sun and was satisfied that his timing was okay.

After a long and zigzag course up the slopes he reached what he fully expected to find—another and somewhat broader trail running east by west on a shallow bench. This trail was also ancient and beaten deeper into the stubborn soil. He was pretty sure that it would lead to the valley not far east of El Paso.

Dismounting, he studied the ground intently for some distance, and arrived at the conclusion that shod horses had passed that way, headed west, only a few hours before.

"It's them," he told Shadow as he remounted. "My hunch was a straight one; they turned west, leaving the posse to go skalleyhooting north. No, the posse did not turn west; not enough prints to indicate that. Looks like all we've got to do is follow this snake track and, if we have luck, perhaps catch up with them when they make camp for the night, which I figure they're almost sure to do. Then we'll see."

"Uh-huh, those that live will see," Shadow's derisive snort seemed to answer. "Only, tackling odds like that, you've got a mighty good chance of not seeing. Oh, well, you've done just such loco things before and somehow managed to scrape through; perhaps you will this time, only I'm not betting on it."

Slade's reply to this burst of equine pessimism was a chuckle. He rode on west with an untroubled mind.

The sun slanted down the sky, its gold slowly turning to red as it neared the horizon. The level rays colored twigs and branches to the ominous hue of congealing blood. And still the old trail curved and twisted westward. Gradually, however, it developed a slight northern trend which Slade found disquieting. In fact, he grew dubious. If the darn thing kept on veering it would not lead to the Rio Grande Valley but would end up in the New Mexico hills. Which was not what he expected the outlaws had in mind. He had deduced that their plan would be to reach the level ground west of El Paso and then slip into the city one or two at a time so as not to attract any attention. Later they would rejoin and continue their western trek.

Then when he was getting quite bothered over the turn events appeared to be taking, he reached a point where the trail forked. One branch continued west by slightly north, the other, narrower and less beaten also ran west but with a slight southerly slant.

Slade again dismounted and studied the ground. The adamantine surface of the main trail retained no impressions of horses' iron, but on the slightly softer surface of the left branch he discovered a print or two, undoubtedly fresh.

"This is it, horse," he said as he swung into the saddle. "They turned off here. This track veers south to reach the valley floor. Looks like my hunch was a straight one, after all."

With intensified vigilance, Slade rode the twisty trail. The outlaws might well be miles ahead of him, but he could not afford to gamble that they were. They might also have halted at a favorable spot to make camp for the night. If they had and he came upon them suddenly, he'd very likely pay with his life for the blunder. They wouldn't want anybody to learn that they had ridden west instead of north and would take no chances on the word of their presence being carried to El Paso before they arrived there.

And his only hope for success crowning his hazardous plan lay in surprise. Even then it would be a desperate venture with the slightest slip guaranteeing failure. But El Halcon had outfaced desperate odds before and he rode on fairly sanguine as to the result if he could force a showdown on his own terms.

For a while he spotted occasional hoof prints where a softer patch of ground was in evidence; but the sun was now touching the western horizon and the shadows were curdling beneath the thick growth. Soon the gloom was so deep that marks on the trail were invisible. However, there was no turning off for anybody riding the track and all he had to do was follow its winding course and he must eventually come up with his quarry. That is if they did stop to make camp for the night, as he fully expected they would.

Shadow's hoof beats sounded loud in the great stillness

of the evening hush, the measured thuds echoing back from the encroaching walls of growth like the monotonous reverberation of muffled drums. Slade knew very well that they were not nearly so loud as they seemed to be, but nevertheless he slowed the big black's gait.

The darkness closed down and each dimly seen bend in the trail was ominous with unspoken threat. Slade's pulses quickened and his nerves were unpleasantly tense. From any of those shadowy curves might come a burst of gunfire that he would see but wouldn't hear, lead travelling a bit faster than sound. He berated his overactive imagination and tried to achieve some humor from the situation, not with outstanding success; he was darned jumpy and admitted it.

The miles flowed past under Shadow's hoofs. Overhead the stars bloomed in the sky like silver roses in the garden of the gods; but their feeble gleam barely penetrated into the narrow canyon between the growth. Later there would be a full moon, but it would have to attain considerable height before its beams would shimmer the trail. Meanwhile he must face the darkness that rose before him like an ebon wall, and hope for the best.

Abruptly he pulled Shadow to a halt and sat listening. To his nostrils had come, faint but unmistakeable, the tang of wood smoke.

For long moments he sat motionless; then he sent Shadow forward again, very slowly. The fire that gave off the smoke was still a considerable distance ahead.

As he progressed, the smell of smoke grew more pronounced, until he concluded it would be unwise to proceed further on horse back. Accordingly, he halted Shadow again and dropped to the ground.

"Stay put, feller, till I see just how things stand," he whispered and stole forward on foot, pausing often to peer and listen. After a while he saw a reddish glow ahead. The hellions had made camp, all right, only the camp seemed strangely quiet for nearly a dozen men. Perhaps, however, they had camped sometime ago and were asleep. Which, if so, would be all to the good from his point of view. With increased caution he crept on.

Now the reddish glow streamed across the trail from a gap in the chaparral. Slade hesitated, listening intently. To his ears came an almost inaudible mutter of voices, and a tiny sound as of metal clanking on metal. He hesitated again, then glided into the growth, worming his way through it without the slightest sound. The glow seeped between the twigs and branches, for he was almost up to the as yet hidden fire. With the greatest caution he parted a final fringe of growth, gazed through the opening, and murmured a disgusted oath.

FIVE

THE FIRE BURNED BRIGHTLY in a small grass grown clearing where a trickle of water flowed. Nearby, a couple of horses grazed contentedly. And squatting before the fire, preparing a meal, were two Mexicans in steeple sombreros and velvet jackets. Their dark faces showed much Indian blood.

For long moments Slade stood gazing at the scene that was utterly unlike what he had expected. The answer, however, was painfully plain. The outlaw bunch had not turned off at the forks but had continued on the main trail, the hard packed soil of which showed no marks of horses passing. And he had gaily followed the prints on the side trail left by the mounts of the Mexicans, who were very likely heading for the valley or perhaps El Paso. Yes, he had tangled his twine nicely. He hesitated as to whether to return to Shadow and ride back the way he had come. Oh, the devil! He'd lost the trail for the time being by his own stupidity, that was all there was to it. Now the outlaws had many hours start and to hope to overtake them this side of El Paso was foolishness. Well, all he could do was try and pick up the trail again in El Paso, for he was still convinced that the devils were headed west. Might as well stop here for the night, if the gents from mañana land proved agreeable, which they very likely would. His mind made up, he stepped from the growth.

The Mexicans jerked their heads up and stared as Slade's tall figure loomed in the firelight.

"Howdy?" he greeted. "Smelled your coffee."

The Mexicans appeared somewhat taken aback by his sudden appearance, which was not unnatural, but quickly regained their composure.

"Buenas noches, Señor," replied one, a stocky, broad-

27

shouldered individual. "The coffee? Ha! it is to the boil. Will not you share a cup with us?"

"Be pleased to do so," Slade accepted.

"Felipe, the pot," said the speaker. His companion plucked the bubbling pot from the fire and filled a tin cup to the brim, which the other passed to Slade with a courteous bow.

"Gracias," Slade said; but as he accepted the cup his black brows drew together slightly, although his face remained impassive. The keen eyes of El Halcon had noticed something.

However, he squatted beside the fire, facing his hosts, and sipped his coffee unconcernedly.

The stocky man spoke again, in the somewhat halting and stilted English common to the Mission-taught Mexican. "The food," he said, "will soon be ready and there is plenty for all, is it not so, Felipe?"

"Si," the other, taller but of slighter build, replied. "There is the great plenty. You will partake with us, Señor?"

"Guess I'd be loco to say no," Slade answered. "Am beginning to feel sort of lank. I'll call my horse."

The Mexicans glanced at each other as he stood up and whistled a loud, clear note. But they broke into unfeigned admiration as with a drumming of hoofs Shadow appeared, snorting inquiringly.

"The beautiful caballo!" exclaimed the stocky man.

"Si, the caballo most wonderful!" said the other.

"He'll do," Slade said briefly, and with seeming carelessness removed the rig, just "happening" to always face the pair by the fire. He unstrapped his tight blanket roll from behind the cantle, shook it out and spread it on the ground, dropping his saddle beside it for a pillow. Then he returned to the fire and accepted the plate of food handed him with a bow.

Slade ate slowly and with relish. No matter what else he might be, Felipe was a darn good cook.

"You go to the valley, Señor?" asked the stocky man, who said his name was Ralpho.

"Yes," Slade replied. "I came down from the north. Was told this track leads to the El Paso trail; I figure on making El Paso."

"Si, it joins the El Paso trail at the foot of the hills,"

nodded Ralpho. "Felipe and I cross the valley to Mejico."

Slade nodded, and for some time they ate in silence. He knew that his companions, while making every effort to conceal the fact, were covertly studying him. Which under the circumstances was not unnatural. They were wondering who the devil he was and what was the meaning of his sudden and mysterious appearance.

Well, let them wonder. What interested him was the conclusion at which they would arrive. From the corners of his eyes he studied them, endeavoring to gain a hint from their facial expressions of what that conclusion might be. He decided to try a little conversation.

"These trails appear not to be much travelled," he commented.

"Not now," replied Ralpho, "but in the old days the Indios travelled them much. Now they are seldom used except by such as Felipe and myself, who come from the mines to the east to visit our homeland."

He paused to chew meditatively for a moment, his eyes gazing past Slade.

"Si, usually but by a miner or two," he repeated, "but today many caballeros rode the upper trail, which is strange."

"Yes?" Slade prompted.

"Si," answered Ralpho. "Felipe and myself were riding the upper trail where it forks when we heard behind us caballos coming with swiftness, many caballos. It is sometimes not good to meet swiftly riding caballeros on these lonely trails, or to be overtaken by them, so Felipe and myself we backed our caballos into the chaparral where we could see and not be seen and waited for those caballeros who rode in haste to pass. They passed, most swiftly, nearly the dozen in number, glancing back over their shoulders at times. We waited until they passed beyond our sight on the upper trail which curves northward to reach, I have been told, New Mexico this side of El Paso. As to the truth of that I cannot say, having never needed to ride the upper trail past the forks."

"Ranches up there to the north, I understand," Slade observed. "Quite likely they were a bunch of cowhands taking a short cut."

"Doubtless the señor is right," Ralpho agreed politely.

Slade offered to help with the dishes, which were

washed in the little stream near the fire, but the offer was courteously declined.

"You are our guest," said Ralpho, which he apparently considered explanation enough. The silent Felipe nodded agreement.

After the utensils were stored in saddle pouches, Ralpho and Felipe spread their blankets near the fire a short distance from where Slade had bedded down.

"It is good to rest after a long day of riding," remarked the former as he stretched out.

Slade also lay down and to all appearances was quickly fast asleep. The full moon was peeping over the crest of the chaparral and soon the clearing was almost daylight bright. Slade lay without sound or motion, his slitted eyes fixed on the two forms which also lay motionless. With every sense stretched to hair-trigger alertness he waited and watched.

The moon rose higher. The great clock in the sky wheeled westward. An owl whined querulously and was answered by the irritated yipping of a coyote. Far off a night bird whistled a plaintive note. The white moonlight crept across the clearing, edging the grass heads with pulsing silver, the tiny shadow of each blade done in cool ebony. Bird and beast ceased their calling and nothing blunted the keen edge of the silence, for even the horses had ceased to crop and stood motionless in sleep. Just as motionless were the two shadowy forms stretched out but a few yards from where El Halcon lay.

Slade's nerves were tightening unbearably. His eyes ached with strain. His muscles were tensed. But his brain was clear and cold, ready to instantly react to whatever message his senses might flash to it.

A full hour crept along the tightly drawn wire of suspense, each crawling minute an eon in itself. And there was movement, slow, stealthy movement as the two forms eased to a sitting position. The swarthy blur of faces turned in Slade's direction. He caught the deadly gleam of shifted metal.

Slade's right hand moved, a wisping flicker too swift for the eye to follow. Even as the two gun muzzles swung toward him, he fired, again, and again, and again.

A shriek knifed through the thunder of the reports, and

a hollow groan. Then answering shots blazed. Back and forth gushed the spears of yellow flame, paled by the shuddering moonlight. A slug tore through the leg of his overalls, another ripped his shirt sleeve and grained the flesh of his arm. Then abruptly he realized that across the narrow strip of grass was only silence. He peered through the swirling smoke wreaths at the still forms sprawled on the tumbled blankets.

For long moments he lay motionless, ready for instant action, then cautiously got to his feet, his cocked gun covering the two "Mexicans." Neither moved and he strode forward a couple of steps, holstering his Colt. Both were satisfactorily dead.

Bending over, he gripped Ralpho's shirt front and ripped it open. The skin of Ralpho's chest gleamed white in the moonlight. Felipe's ripped shirt also showed body skin startlingly pale in contrast to his swarthy face.

SIX

SLADE THREW A FEW CHUNKS of wood on the smoldering fire, which instantly blazed up brightly. He set the half-full coffee pot amid the flames, straightened up and rolled a cigarette.

"Smart," he told Shadow, who was snorting inquiringly. "Mighty smart. They acted the part to perfection in speech, gestures, everything. But they made one little slip. Not much of a slip, but enough to get them their come-uppance. With the stain with which they darkened their faces, they also smeared the palms of their hands. The palms of a Mexican's hands, of an Indian's, or a Negro's even, for that matter, are pinkish, not dark brown like the backs. When that hellion passed me the cup of coffee I noticed it and knew he was no more a Mexican than I am."

He paused, while Shadow looked expectant.

"One thing is sure for certain, horse," he resumed, "whoever heads that infernal outfit has got brains and knows how to use them. He misses mighty few bets. That stunt at the Hueco bank was clever. Not exactly new— I know of a somewhat similar episode that was pulled once—but with a few original twists that were effective." He paused to flip the coffee pot from the fire, root out one of the tin cups and fill it to the brim.

"Yes," he continued, speaking his thoughts to the horse, as is a habit with men who ride much alone and look upon their mounts as comrades who understand. "Yes, he doesn't miss many bets. He figured there was just a possibility of the pursuit not being fooled into believing he continued on north to New Mexico, and with his horses heavily laden he feared a pursuing posse. So evidently being familiar with the section, he sent his two 'Mexicans' down the south trail, leaving plain prints on its surface. The pursuing posse, if one had followed the upper trail, would have blundered down this one, just as I did, and when they finally caught up with the gents who left the prints, they would have found two 'harmless Mexicans' making camp for the night. Plumb perfect, except for that one little slip. Well, the outlaw brand always makes them, one way or another; so here's hoping they make another soon. Perhaps we'll be able to learn something in El Paso. And anyhow we did for two of the sidewinders, which helps a mite."

What he did not stress to Shadow was his own uncanny knack for noticing the smallest details and properly evaluating them. That, however, was what made Walt Slade the most feared as well as the most fearless of that illustrious and intrepid body of law enforcement officers, the Texas Rangers!

Glancing at the stars, he decided that he still had time for a few hours sleep before daylight. Before lying down, however, he gave the bodies of the two outlaws a careful examination. Their pockets revealed nothing but a large sum of money, which he replaced, and various trinkets that identified them as former cowhands, although their hands showed no recent marks of rope or branding iron. The two horses bore meaningless Mexican brands and the rigs were of good quality but ordinary. The horses he would leave to fend for themselves, knowing that they could do so and would eventually reach the lower grasslands where somebody would pick them up. After dropping a little more wood on the fire he lay down and slept soundly until the rose and gold of the dawn brightened the eastern sky.

There were still some provisions in the outlaws' saddle pouches so he cooked breakfast and warmed up the coffee before moving on. The two bodies he covered with the blankets and left them to poison the coyotes and buzzards. Then with a final glance around the clearing he got the rig on Shadow and rode west by south through a world all glorious with morning.

Shortly the trail ceased its southward trend and ran due west for many miles, then veering abruptly south to pass that strange area known as the Hueco Tanks, a great clutter of giant rocks which lie scattered in wild confusion over a region of nearly a mile long by half a mile wide. Within this rock-bound natural fortress various tribes, from prehistoric men up to the era of occupation of the section by the Apaches, had villages secure from hostile bands. Wind and rain erosion cut many waterholes in the soft granite. Slade noted caves and narrow over-hung ravines that offered good protection from the elements.

Shadow enjoyed a good drink from one of the waterholes and Slade had a swig himself. After which he rode on and reached the broad El Paso trail.

He rode slowly along the well-travelled road, enjoying a period of relaxation which was welcome after the recent hectic activity to which he had been subjected. And as he rode, he endeavored to make plans for the future.

Slade rather doubted that the outlaws would stop at El Paso, where the authorities had of course been notified of the Hueco murder and robbery and would keep a sharp lookout for the perpetrators of the outrage. But that daring and clever outfit might well be expected to do the unexpected. So he resolved to spend a little time in El Paso in the hope of picking up some crumbs of information. Better not to miss any bets. He still believed that the owlhoots would continue west, but he was not sure. The wild mountains of New Mexico afforded sanctuary for evildoers and the bunch might decide to make for that desolate terrain and lie low a while. Or they might think it advisable to cross the Rio Grande to Mexico where there were more and equally inhospitable mountains.

The lovely blue dusk was sifting down from the hills when he arrived at the city. Which for nearly four centuries, in one form or another, has stood by "the Pass" that is the lowest natural gateway in that region of deserts and mountains where the westermost tip of Texas touches the borders of Mexico and New Mexico.

He stabled his horse and found accommodations for himself at a nearby hotel. After a bath and a shave, which helped a lot, he sallied forth in quest of something to eat and possible information. He was acquainted in El Paso, as a Ranger in some quarters, as El Halcon the notorious owlhoot too smart to get caught, in others. By one route or the other he hoped to learn whatever, if anything, there was to be learned.

SEVEN

SLADE SPENT TWO DAYS and a night in El Paso and learned nothing. It appeared the bunch had avoided the town, presumably continuing west into New Mexico. The following morning he followed his hunch that they did. Crossing the state line, he slipped his Ranger badge from its hiding place and regarded it a moment.

"Well, horse," he said to Shadow, "all the authority I have now is what hangs at my belt; but I've a notion that will be enough. It'll have to be."

He stowed the badge back in its secret pocket and rode on. He rode slowly for now the bunch could have turned in any direction—into the northern mountains, south into Mexico, or on west. He still believed the owlhoots were headed west.

He had covered less than fifty miles into New Mexico when his judgment was once more confirmed. At a little village where he spent a night he learned that an outlaw band had held up a stage, killing the guard and seriously wounding the driver. The bunch tallied with the rather vague description given him by the rancher-grape grower east of El Paso. Both the rancher and the villagers agreed that the man who appeared to be the leader of the band was tall and powerfully built, with black or very dark brown hair. The others appeared to be an average lot of hard characters with nothing outstanding about them.

Not much to go on, Slade was forced to admit. Plenty of big men with dark hair.

Slade thoughtfully digested what he had learned, and arrived at a conclusion that did not appear to dovetail with the facts, so far as he heard them.

"The devils went into the north hills, with the sheriff and his posse after them," his informant said. "He'll get 'em. Sheriff Martin is a smart hombre."

35

However, Slade had a hunch that in this particular instance the sheriff was not being a "smart" hombre. He was still convinced that the outlaws were headed west. They would cover their tracks in the hill country and circle back south. When he left the village the following morning, Slade did not turn north but continued west on that trail which had once been a famous stagecoach route, but was now lonely and not much travelled.

Thirty miles west of the village he knew he had again been right. Standing beside the trail was a patient burro with a rifled pack strapped to its back. In the trail lay a dead man who wore miner's clothes. He had been shot through the head, murdered for the gold he had toiled to dig out of the stubborn hills. Slade placed the body to one side, with the hands folded on the breast; he felt he had no time to bury it, and somebody would find it and give it decent interment. He removed the pack from the burro's back and turned the little animal loose to graze. Then he rode on, his face bleak.

Further developments indicated that the band was making a specialty of robbing lone miners and prospectors. Twice more before he crossed the New Mexico state line into Arizona, Slade discovered grisly evidence of its passing.

Nearly a month had elapsed since that fatal night in the valley east of El Paso but he was confident he was on the right track. And then in the broad San Simon Valley he lost the trail completely. The killers could have turned in any direction. They might have holed up in the Chiricahuas across the valley, Curly Bill Brocius's old hangout, or in the Dragoons that shadowed Tombstone, or the Huachucas to the southwest. He spent a fruitless week in Tombstone, another in Bisbee, a third in Benson. It looked like a dead end.

Then Slade decided to again follow a hunch. He headed straight west for the California line, which he reached after a long and hard ride that consumed two more weeks. For more than two months he had been trailing the elusive band, with no results. Captain Jim might well be believing that he had actually decided to bridge the Pacific. He chuckled at the thought and rode on into the grim desolation of the Mohave Desert. He planned to cross the southwest tip of the arid wasteland,

heading for the bustling and fast growing town of Los
Angeles or perhaps turning north, depending on what
information he might be able to pick up. He still followed
the old stage route, the most logical course and the one
that would, he thought, be used by the outlaws if they
really were in front of him and headed for some point
in California.

It was on his third day into the desert that the storm
swept up from the southwest. Slade gazed at the ominous
saffron sky with some apprehension. That sky could mean
trouble. The crossing under favorable conditions was no
light matter. Already his water was exhausted, the last
gill or two in his canteens having gone to moisten Shadow's lips a couple of hours before. As yet, the air was
clear, but far to the south was what appeared to be a
curtain rising from the thin, fine line of the horizon.
That "curtain," Slade knew, was dust and sand rising on
the wings of the wind.

Even as Slade gazed, long banners and streamers thrust
out from its wavering crest, advancing, retreating, tossing
wildly. Plenty of wind coming his way. He swept the
desert with his keen glance. To the west, perhaps eight
or ten miles distant, was a sudden upheaval that had the
appearance of a grim and mighty fortress rising from
the desert floor. He studied it a moment, fixing the location in his mind. His plainsman's instinct for distance
and direction would lead him to the formation in even
the darkest night. And very quickly it would be "night," so
far as being able to see anything a hundred yards or so
away was concerned. Slade had had enough experience
with desert storms to be sure of that.

"But those rocks over there must mean canyons and
gulleys," he told Shadow. "And they could mean water.
Jump along, horse, let's go and see."

Far to the southwest the San Bernardino Mountains
lay, a misty purple shadow on the horizon, not yet wholly
obscured by the rising dust, while almost due west the
Sierra Madres started up from the fringe of the desert,
their rugged crests looking across the intervening miles to
the blue waters of the Pacific.

On came the storm. The sky darkened, filled with
dancing particles that caught glints of sunlight. Overhead
a hollow roar developed, a sinister tearing sound, as if the

envelope of the universe was being ripped apart. And
spiralling down that ladder of changing tones came the
Mohave's dreaded furnace wind.

Almost instantly the temperature rose many degrees.
Dimly through the swirling dust clouds, the great California sun shone a deep, weird magenta color as the pall
of yellow dust shifted and billowed under the tearing
fingers of the wind. Slade, face stung by flying sand and
bits of gravel, bent his head and rode on, blindly steering
for the rocky hills that could mean sanctuary.

At times the fierce breath of the wind would lessen, the
air would clear and the savage landscape would flash out
in all its wild hideousness and wilder beauty. But high
in the air the yellow dust cloud still hung and through
it that weird sun, like an orange-red moon seen through
haze, seemed to focus its rays as through a burning glass
on horse and rider.

As Shadow slogged ahead, blowing and panting, reeling
drunkenly at times, Slade began to grow distinctly worried. They couldn't take much more of this without
water. His tongue was swelling, his lips cracking; his
eyes were alternately blinded by the flying dust and
dazzled by the red glare of the sun. There was a throbbing
at his temples, a dull ringing in his ears. It seemed the
blistering heat was sucking the blood from his veins. His
skin was dry, his body like a hot ember.

And Shadow, he knew, was in little better case. If the
black horse happened to fall, in all probability he would
never rise again. Slade set his jaw and peered ahead during
a moment when the air cleared a little. He was sure they
had very nearly covered the distance to the rock outcropping he had sighted before the storm broke.

Again the gale strengthened and the dust cloud swooped
down. Many minutes passed before it rose again. And as
the air cleared a bit, Slade breathed a deep sigh of relief.
Directly ahead loomed a jumble of stony rises, soaring
pinnacles and beetling cliffs. And gashing the floor of the
desert like the ragged wound made by a gigantic spear
was a vast amphitheatre which was really the sunken
mouth of a canyon that bored into the craggy range. Its
depths were possibly wooded, and if so he might discover
water. Before the cloud lowered again, Slade sent Shadow
down the slope that led into the canyon, close to the

steadily rising cliff which was the south wall of the gorge. Another slight lull in the storm and he found the gentle slope had ended, replaced by a series of terraces that stepped downward one onto another, with slopes between. He could see but a short distance, however; the bottom of the amphitheatre and what was beyond invisible because of the sheets of dust rushing upward from the huge funnel.

Crowding Shadow close against the rock wall, Slade pulled up and debated what was best to do. Finally he decided to leave the horse where he was, sheltered somewhat by the cliff which already soared upward far above his head. It was cooler than in the full blast of the sun beating through the dust cloud and the black wouldn't be too uncomfortable. He swung from the saddle, gave the glossy neck a pat and began the descent into the eerie and terrible abyss of flying yellow shadows.

He drew near the bottom of the bowl. The gale roared overhead and the place was shrouded in a strange yellow twilight. The heat pouring into the cup was even more intense than that which shimmered above its rim. But into the pit of the amphitheatre, he could now see, emptied the true mouth of the canyon boring into the hills.

Suddenly he was conscious of a sound rising on the wing of the wind, piercing its shriek and roar, a strange rumbling, grating sound punctuated by louder bumps and sharp squeaking creaks as of wood tight against wood. What in blazes! He moved forward and abruptly halted, staring into the dust-streaked depths.

The pit of the amphitheatre was level, a sort of round pocket floored with hard-packed sand. One curving side was walled by a ledge of crumbling rock which was a shelving continuation of the canyon wall proper.

On the floor of the pocket were brush roofs set on poles, evidently erected for shade. One farthest from Slade housed packs and other odds and ends of a camp. The other and larger of the two was roughly square in shape, the brush roof supported by stout posts. From under it came the rumble of rocks, the harsh squeaking and now and again the metallic clang of shovels.

Under the brush an *arrastra* was in operation, that most primitive of stamp mills, by means of which the early Spaniards ground the ore they dug from the California hills and extracted the gold.

In the center of the brush-roof enclosure a pit had been dug, lined and floored with flat stones. An upright beam was set in the middle of the pit and fastened to the roof. Cross-beams were attached to the upright and from these cross-beams dragged heavy rocks held by chains. A long pole, set at right-angles to the upright beam and secured to it, extended beyond the edge of the pit at about four feet from the ground. The upright beam, set in sockets above, could be revolved by means of this pole. The cross-beams dragged the heavy rocks over the stone floor of the pit, crushing the ore that lay on the floor and grinding it to powder.

Usually the upright beam of the *arrastra* was revolved by a horse or mule hitched to the horizontal pole; but in this case no quadruped strained and sweated in the infernal heat of that ghastly hole. Roped to the pole, blind, reeling, dizzy with fatigue, their blackened tongues protruding from their cracked and bleeding lips, two grizzle-haired, gray-bearded men staggered around and around the awful treadmill, throwing their weight against the pole, dragging the heavy stones over the broken ore. And not from choice. Not even the compelling lust for gold that makes men mad could have caused human beings to endure such torment.

Seated just outside the radius of the pole was a blocky, powerful individual with cruel eyes and a bushy black beard. He held in his hand a heavy quirt with which he lashed the bare backs of the staggering oldsters as their dreary round brought them within reach of his sinewy arm. He roared curses and obscenities as they stumbled past him, punctuated with the crack of his lash on bloody flesh.

Two other men were carrying ore from the ledge, dumping and shoveling it into the pit. They paused from time to time to wipe their streaming faces, curse the heat and add their jeers to the bearded man's as the two old prospectors lurched past.

The dust swirled down, writhing in and out under the brush roof, taking on fantastic shapes that pulsed and glowed with unholy color. Under its concealing veil, Slade took two long strides forward.

Abruptly the saffron cloud whirled high. Once more the pit was clear of flying particles and the bearded man suddenly jumped from his seat with a startled oath. The other two straightened, shovels gripped in tense hands, staring at Slade's tall form standing just inside the shadow of the brush roof. The bearded man let out a roaring curse.

"What the devil you doing here?" he bawled. "Get out, and get out fast!"

Slade continued to gaze at the staggering prospectors stumbling in their never-ceasing round. His cold eyes moved the merest trifle to include the bearded man and his two companions. Without moving his head he spoke.

"Don't you think it would be a good idea to spell those two gents now and then, before they tumble over?" he asked, his voice deceptively mild.

The bearded man seemed for the moment bereft of speech. He glared, his cruel reptilian mouth writhing crookedly to expose yellow snags of teeth. Then he let out an enraged howl and clubbing the heavy quirt, he rushed at Slade, astonishingly agile for his bulk.

Slade waved aside slightly to avoid the vicious blow struck at his head. As the quirt glanced harmlessly past his shoulder, his left hand flashed out and up. A fist hard as a block of iron caught the bearded man squarely on the angle of the jaw with a smack that mixed with the bellow of the wind.

Lifted clean off his feet, the bearded man cleared the edge of the arrastra pit and shot downward. His head hit the rock floor with a sodden crunching sound, his big body writhed for an instant, stiffened, and was still. With yells of rage his two companions went for the guns hanging at their hips. Dust particles danced to the roar of six-shooters.

Guns rock-steady against his hips, Walt Slade peered through the smoke and dust at the two figures sprawled on the edge of the pit. His glance dropped to the bearded man, oozing blood over the crushed ore, then centered on the two old prospectors who, eyes dazed and unbelieving, sagged against the pole to which they were tethered.

"Any more of the devils around?" Slade asked.

"That's all," one croaked.

Slade holstered his guns, drew his knife. A couple of slashes freed the captives, who slumped to the ground.

"Water!" They pointed with shaking fingers to a canteen hanging on one of the roof poles.

Slade secured the canteen and gave each a couple of swallows. With gentle force he restrained them from gulping more.

"You oldtimers should know better," he chided. "You know what too much water all at once will do to you in your condition. Here, you can each have one more swig, and that's all for the time being. Now isn't there someplace around here that's cooler than this infernal hole?"

"Up the canyon," one panted. "You're right about the water, son, but when you've been plumb starved for it for days like us fellers have, you ain't got no sense when you get your hands on some. Help me up, will you?"

The old fellow was full of a sort of surly courage. With Slade's assistance he gained his feet, gripping a roof pole for support. His companion also struggled to come erect but could only flounder helplessly till Slade lifted him and held him steady till he was able to stand alone. Stepping back, he drew his guns, ejected the empty shells and replaced them with fresh cartridges. Then he sheathed the big Colts and studied the prospectors.

"How come you were roped to that pole, and who are those three gents who have gone from among us?" he asked.

The old men started as if awakening from a bad dream. Their eyes widened and an expression of overpowering fear spasmed their features.

"We—we got to get out of here pronto," stuttered the older of the pair. "Those hellions were part of Joaquin Murrieta's outfit and there's more of them hereabouts somewhere. They show up every now and then to relieve the ones working in this hole. If they catch us here we're all done for."

Slade stared at mention of California's most notorious bandit leader.

"What are you talking about?" he asked. "Joaquin Murrieta's been dead for years. California Ranger Henderson killed him in Priest Valley."

"Not this Joaquin Murrieta!" chattered the prospector. "He's plumb alive and kicking."

Slade shrugged. "Probably some brush-popping owlhoot trading on a name."

"But what if some of 'em come back and catch us here?" asked the prospector. He was shaking with terror at the prospect; so was his companion. Slade did not look very much impressed.

"If they do, they'll very likely stay here," he said. He glanced up at the dust cloud swirling above the bowl, let his eyes fall to the rock-walled canyon and shook his head.

"Pretty bad outside," he observed. "A lot worse than down here. Is there water in the canyon?"

The oldsters nodded mutely.

"Then we're staying right here till the storm breaks," Slade said. "I'll get my horse and then you can lead the way into that canyon and the water; afterward we'll talk."

The old man opened his lips to protest again, then his gaze rested on the steady gray eyes under their black brows and he closed them again and turned away.

"Come on, Pete," he said to his companion.

Slade faced the bowl rim and whistled a loud clear note. A moment later there was a clatter of hoofs and Shadow hove into view, snorting a profane opinion of the dust, the heat, and everything in general. Slade chuckled and followed the two prospectors, Shadow pacing beside him.

Once in the canyon proper, there was very little dust and the heat was decidedly abated. The hollow roar of the gale was now high above the towering rock walls, with only vagrant puffs and swirls penetrating to the depths. The prospectors led the way to a substantial lean-to built against the cliff face

"Here's where Pete and me had our camp before those devils jumped our claim," he exclaimed. "Plenty of chuck here—we had some and they brought in more. We'll start coffee b'ilin' and something cooking right away. I'm Sam Conklin, son, and this other old coot is Pete Trevis; we come originally from Nevada."

Slade supplied his own name. "From Texas," he added. He made no mention as to why he happened to be in California.

EIGHT

THERE WAS WATER in the canyon. It looked like vinegar, was hot, and did not taste as water should taste.

"But it ain't poison and it'll keep you going; not at all bad made into coffee. And I reckon your horse will find those patches of grass over there better than nothing," said Trevis.

Slade nodded agreement and got the rig off Shadow, who had a drink, rolled a couple of times and then began cropping grass.

A little later his master and the prospectors went to work on a bountiful meal quickly thrown together by Conklin who, he explained, was once a ranch cook.

"And now," Slade said, "suppose you tell me just what happened, how you came to be roped to that pole and what you know about the gent who calls himself Joaquin Murrieta."

The two oldsters glanced at each other. "You tell him," said Trevis, who appeared by nature taciturn.

"Okay," Conklin replied. "You see, Slade, it was like this. We're prospectors and we figured there ought to be gold somewhere in this mess of rocks. We were right. That ledge out there is mighty rich ore. Hard to work and one devil of a place to work in, but we were doing all right before those horned toads dropped in here and jumped our claim. We were using our burros to work the arrastra, but those darn mules always drift up the canyon quite a ways during the night to where the grass is better. Some trouble to round 'em up, but we figure the poor critters have a right to nose out better provender if they can. It was early in the morning when those sidewinders swooped down on us like forty hen hawks on a settin' quail. We hadn't gone looking for the burros yet. The snake-blooded devils didn't bother to round up the

44

burros. They just hitched Pete and me to the pole and made us do the grinding. Seemed to really enjoy working us to death. I've a notion we wouldn't have lasted more than another day or so if you hadn't happened along when you did. What with being drove like mules and whipped all the time and given hardly any water and less to eat, we were pretty close to our finish. No use trying to thank you for what you did, but maybe we can sort of even up things in another way. We'll talk about that before we pull out."

"No thanks due," Slade smiled. "It was a pleasure. But what about the Murrieta gent? Who is he, and what is he?"

"Nobody 'pears to know just who he is," Conklin replied. "He's just a name—but it's a name folks in this section are more scared of than they are of the Devil. Guess because they ain't sure there is a Devil, while there ain't no doubt about theré being a Murrieta. He runs a bunch that robs and murders, and don't leave no witnesses. Been operating in the section for a couple years and more now. Drop out of sight for a while every now and then, but always show up again and pull some more hellishness. He's got folks scared, with plenty of reason."

Slade nodded thoughtfully. There was nothing new about the story—the same old owlhoot tactics. Get people frightened and afraid to fight back. Curly Bill Brocius did it in Arizona. Kingfisher and his bunch in Texas. The Doc Skurlock-Billy the Kid gang in New Mexico. Merciless killers who ruled through terror. And all met their end at the hands of intrepid, straight-shooting law officers who didn't scare. Slade was not impressed, but he was interested.

The prospectors were perking up fast. They had eaten like starving men and downed vast quantities of coffee. Now with their pipes going full blast, they were beginning to look fit for anything. They were sturdy old men and despite the fearful treatment they had received at the hands of the claim jumpers, they were but little affected by the hardships they had been forced to endure. But they were anxious to leave the canyon as soon as the storm let up a bit.

"Most any time now some of the bunch will show up to relieve those three you downed," they explained to Slade. "Hard to tell how many of the devils will come along. There were seven or eight one time when they brought in a couple of loads of provisions."

Slade did not argue the point. No sense in bucking heavy odds when it wasn't necessary. The tradition of the Texas Rangers held that a Ranger should be courageous, but that courage needed to be backed by common sense, and foolhardiness was not bravery.

While Trevis cleaned up the camp, Conklin hurried up the canyon to locate the strayed burros.

"Chances he won't have to go over far," said Trevis. "Good grass about a mile up the canyon; that's where they'll be." He began packing the utensils and hauling a number of plumb pokes from a hole in the cliff.

Slade browsed about amid the chaparral that clothed the canyon floor and brought back a handful of leaves which he bruised with a stone to a moist pulp. Before he had finished, Conklin appeared driving four lop-eared, deceptively meek burros. Slade told the oldsters to remove the shirts they had donned. He applied the juicy pulp to their lacerated backs.

"Learned the trick from a Karankawa Indian," he explained. "The Kranks, not many of them left, were the herb and poison people of the Texas Indians. Not much they didn't know about such things. This poultice will take the soreness out and help the cuts to heal."

"Feels fine, even though it does sting a mite," Conklin admitted. "And now, son," he added as he replaced his shirt, "in those pokes is a hefty helpin' of dust and nuggets. It's share and share alike with the three of us."

But Slade smilingly shook his head. "Much obliged, but I've got a few pesos," he said. "Enough to see me through till I tie onto a job of riding or something."

Both Conklin and Trevis looked disappointed. "Well, if you won't, you won't," said the latter. "But if things don't go right, we'll be expecting you to look us up any time you need a helpin' hand. We're going to salt away part of this gold to have it ready in case you want it. If it wasn't for you, we wouldn't have any of it. Nor any use for it, either."

Slade's cold, reckless eyes were kindly as he smiled down at the two old fellows from his great height.

"It was a real pleasure to do a favor for real folks," he

said. "Well, everything ready? Then suppose we make a start."

"Okay," said Conklin. "We'll head for town."

"Town?"

"Uh-huh, a mite more than sixty miles to the southwest from here is a pretty good town. Got a funny name—they call it the City of the Angels."

"Los Angeles, eh?" Slade interpolated in an amused voice.

"That's right," nodded Conklin, "City of the Angels. But I ain't ever seen any angels there, leastwise not the kind they say live in the Good Place up above. Some salty sections thereabouts. Down in the street the Mexicans call *La Calle*, for instance."

"The Alley," Slade translated.

"That's right, where such nice gents as Crooked Nose Smith and Cherokee Bob used to hang out. I've a notion you could turn over the upper crust of hell there with one swipe of a spade.

"But she's a nice town just the same," he added with a chuckle. "Shootings, cuttings, good likker; gambling houses on every corner next to the saloon—three or four of them in between corners—dance halls, pretty girls who ain't too particular—lots of interesting things. Come along with us, son, if you haven't got any place in particular to head for."

"I believe I will," Slade replied.

"Good! Let's go!" said Conklin. He hesitated a moment, then, "There's just one thing that bothers me a mite," he admitted. "They say the City of the Angels is the real hangout and headquarters for the Murrieta gang."

"From what you told me, it appears they hang out most anywhere in this section," Slade pointed out. "So let's not bother our heads about them until and if we run into them."

Sunset was flaming in the west when they passed the ghastly pit and the stiffened corpses of the three outlaws and climbed the steeply sloping walls of the amphitheatre. The wind had died and the desert was deathly still. From the shadowy depths of the canyon they had quitted came, faint with distance, the mournful, lonely plaint of a hunting wolf. It was the very voice of the wastelands, calling the wanderer to join in that fierce game with the wilderness, where the forfeit is death.

Slade was silent, preoccupied. The recent hectic happenings had given him considerable to think about. In his own mind, he leaned toward associating the Murrieta bunch with the robbers and killers he was trailing. There was an intriguing similarity in method; they made a specialty of preying on prospectors, and they certainly did not leave any witnesses. Could the two be one and the same?

But after due reflection he dismissed the notion as hardly feasible. Evidently the Murrieta band was a local outfit which had been operating in this corner of California for a considerable length of time, not a bunch putting distance between themselves and Texas. And all owlhoot depredations followed a common pattern with only minor differences of detail. But Los Angeles was an up-and-coming town that had not as yet settled down to a peaceful, law-abiding existence and could be attractive to his quarry. Very probably it was. Just as likely they would make for the southern town rather than turn north to San Francisco or Sacramento.

Well, he had headed west on a hunch, and it seemed to him he was still following the right course. And Los Angeles was nearly as far west as he could hope to get without bridging the Pacific, so he'd give Los Angeles a whirl.

With his mind made up, he gave himself over to enjoying the ride through the comparatively cool night air under the glittering stars. Beside him plodded the old prospectors, driving their loaded burros. It was nearly dawn when they made camp beside a trickle of water that ran from beneath a clump of rock and slept soundly in the shade of an overhang until well past noon, starting out again at sunset. They travelled mostly at night, taking it easy, and just as the third day's sun was setting they reached the City of the Angels.

"I'm beginning to believe you were right in your estimate of this pueblo," Slade remarked to Conklin as they threaded their way through the crowded streets.

"She's a humdinger, all right," Conklin chuckled. "Don't reckon there's another to equal her anywhere. San Francisco is a mite bigger and plenty woolly, but not up to Los Angeles for general hell raising." He added in lower tones:

"And I reckon there are more owlhoots here than any other place on the Pacific coast and points east. In the old days, San Francisco had The Hounds and the Sidney Ducks, but they were tame compared to the specimens they've got here. They come from the gold diggin's in the Sacramento Valley. They come from Mexico. They come in from ships cruising along the coast. They come across from Arizona and New Mexico, and even Texas. All the hellions from Mexico bound for the gold fields up north come along this way and stop off. The town is a plumb natural for them. The wild country is close, and it ain't far—just a short ride—to the Mexico border. Any way they turn it's easy for them to get to hole-in-the-wall hangouts. This Los Angeles town is where the whole kit and kaboodle meet to raise merry hell. And, son, they raise it! I figure this is going to be a big city some day. The second railroad will be here mighty soon and that'll make the town grow. Yes, someday she'll be a big city, and a place for decent folks to live. But now—gentlemen, hush!"

It was indeed a wild and boisterous scene. Sinewy cowboys jostled shoulders with miners in shirts of flaming red, blue, or plaid. Here and there an Indian stalked along with great dignity. Chinese in flapping blouses slithered past on felt-soled sandals. There were Mexican vaqueros from below the Line, their black velvet costumes adorned with much silver. Dance-floor girls flounced along, whisking their skirts, their eyes bold and inviting. It seemed that every man present bristled with deadly weapons.

The strains of music that streamed over the swinging doors of the saloons were punctuated by the jingle of gold pieces, the cheerful clink of bottlenecks on glass rims, the thump of booted feet and the sprightly click of high heels. A gunshot rang out somewhere up the street. An eddy in the crowd there, strident curses.

"Just a mite of an argument," old Pete Trevis observed cheerfully. "There goes one of 'em across the street, I'd say. Reckon the other feller stayed right where he was."

Los Angeles had not yet enjoyed the tremendous land boom that was to achieve national prominence for the City of the Angels, as a result of which the population would increase from 12,000 to 50,000 in little more than two years. As yet, although a hundred years old, it was still a frontier town and plenty salty. But Slade thought that already there were signs of steady and prosperous growth. There were plenty of establishments other than gambling halls and saloons lining the street, all of which appeared to be doing a good business.

The prospectors paused before a golden-blazing square of plate glass.

"That's the Square Deal saloon," Conklin announced. "We'll be dropping in there after we put up our burros back of the Cowman's Hotel. Come on, just around the corner."

Before a ramshackle building on the quieter side street he paused again.

"Here she is," he announced. "We'll sleep here tonight —'long toward morning, I reckon. Want us to sign up for a room for you, too?"

"Not just yet," Slade replied. "I want to look after my horse first and get a bite to eat."

"Keep on going a few doors farther and you'll find a stable," directed Trevis. "Good place. Nice feller runs it, feller named Vergara. Okay, we'll see you in the Square Deal."

Slade had no trouble locating the stable, a clean looking, whitewashed building. A sign over the door read *Meson*, proclaiming that the establishment catered to the wants of both man and beast. The wide door was swung open by a swarthy, smiling young man who was undoubtedly of Mexican extraction but who spoke English.

"Texas, eh?" he remarked as he helped Slade get the rig off Shadow.

"How'd you guess?" Slade smiled, although he knew pretty well how.

"Low-horned saddle with two cinches, a 'trunk strap' instead of whang leather latigos, narrow iron stirrups, sisal rope, split reins—just drop the loose ends to the ground when you want the cayuse to stand; no tieing with a hair rope. You don't see this kind of rig in use west of Texas. I rode there for a spell."

"Good eyes," Slade commented. Vergara grinned and gazed admiringly at Shadow.

"Quite a few folks hereabouts from over Texas way," he observed. "Felipe, the orchestra leader at the Alhambra, the big place down in The Alley, and most of his bunch, come from over there, though I guess they were born south of the Rio Grande. Felipe used to play at a place in El Paso. As you may have noticed, Mexican musicians are a wandering lot—itchy feet, I guess. Felipe and his boys played at the Occidental, Wyatt Earp's saloon in Tombstone, too. Finally drifted over here. Next month or two and you're liable to find them in San Francisco. Can't keep still. There, your horse is all taken care of."

"And he took to you first off, which old Shadow doesn't always do with strangers," Slade remarked. "I figure he'll be safe here."

"Yes, he will be safe," said Vergara, fingering the handle of the huge knife swinging at his belt. He spoke quietly but there was that in his voice that relieved Slade of any anxiety where his mount was concerned.

"Where do you sleep tonight?" Vergara asked, adding a trifle diffidently, "I have rooms over the stalls if you'd like to be close to your horse. They're small, but comfortable and clean. Water and soap in back, if you'd care to wash up a bit."

Slade nodded, and decided that a room over the stalls would doubtless be preferable to one at the Cowman's Hotel, which had struck him as something in the nature of a fleabag.

"That'll be fine," he said. "I'll put my rifle and my pouches in one and then look for something to eat."

"The restaurant diagonally across the street serves good chuck," said Vergara. "Clean, too. Here is a key to the front door, if you happen to come in late. I don't often give them out."

"Thank you," Slade said seriously, appreciating the implied compliment.

NINE

SLADE WASHED, then headed for the restaurant across the street, which was little more than an alley. The little eating house was run by a fat and jolly Mexican who placed an appetizing meal on the table. Slade ate in leisurely fashion, then smoked a couple of cigarettes and lingered over a final cup of coffee.

"Think I'll mosey around the corner and give the town a once-over," he remarked to his host as he paid the bill. "Sort of interesting, judging from what I've seen of it."

"Si, it is very interesting, sometimes too much so for a peace-loving man like myself," the owner replied. "Come again, Señor, you will always be welcome."

Leaving the alley, Slade turned into Main Street and a little later paused before the brilliantly lighted windows of the Square Deal. He pushed through the swinging doors and entered the saloon.

The big room was already crowded and boisterous. Near the far end of the bar he spotted Sam Conklin and Pete Trevis, well on the way to a roaring drunk. Trevis, usually taciturn, let out a whoop of welcome on catching sight of him.

"That's him!" he bellowed to the bartender who was filling their glasses with straight whiskey. "That's the feller who did for three of Murrieta's hellions as easy as flipping a nugget. He's the one I was telling you about.

"Come here, son, and sample a snort of red-eye," he shouted to Slade. "Got desert water beat all hollow, but just about as pizen. Fill 'em up, barkeep! It's my night to howl!"

Slade made his way down the bar. He did not particularly care for the attention directed toward him because of Trevis' bellowed remarks, but the old pelican meant well and was too drunk to exercise judgment. He accepted

52

a drink from Trevis who regarded him owlishly and drank with him, downing the fiery liquor at a gulp. Slade drained his glass and topped it with a second.

"One on the house," announced the bartender in admiring tones. "Anybody who can down two of that stuff without making a face deserves a free snake."

"Pete always gets jabbery after a snort or two, but there ain't no harm in him," Conklin, much the soberer of the two, confided to Slade. "Sort of a way with quiet fellers, I've noticed. Save up on talk and then turn it all loose at once. Nice place, don't you think?"

Slade nodded and eyed the crowded room with interest. As he glanced about, a man sauntered past, nodded to the bartender, gazed keenly down the bar a moment and then made his way to the faro bank, which was doing a booming business.

"That's Dave Lang, who owns the diggin's," said Conklin. "He's a salty hombre but a nice feller and a square-shooter. Runs straight games and don't stand for any foolishness from the help: He's got our gold in his safe in the back room—always handles what we bring in for us—and every ounce will be right there when we want it."

Slade studied the saloonkeeper who, in appearance, he thought, was worthy of more than a casual glance. Tall, broad-shouldered, strikingly handsome, he walked with the grace of a stalking panther. His eyes were jet black and of a strange brilliance, his face dark and mobile with cameo-perfect features. But there was a prominence to his chin and a hard set to his mouth that relieved his face from any trace of effeminacy despite his extreme good looks. His hair, in contrast to his eyes and coloring, was crisply golden, curling back from his high broad forehead. His arms were long and hung loosely from his shoulders. The downward pointing hands gave Slade the impression of spear points at rest.

"Looks like a cold proposition, all right," he agreed with Conklin. "And I'd say he's got something other than bone beneath that yellow hair."

"You're right," Conklin acceded. "Dave sort of sets up to be a first citizen of this town, even though he has been here only a couple of years. Owns this place, the biggest moneymaker in town, and a cow ranch, and an interest in a mine up north in the Sacramento Valley, I've been told.

Goes up there every now and then for a month or so. Rest of the time he's right in the Square Deal, getting to know folks and making friends. Folks say he's going to run for mayor next election. Reckon he'll make it, too, if Amada Fuentes doesn't beat him. Lang has lots of friends, some of 'em among the best people. Lots of folks are for Fuentes, though, even though there are some who don't think overly well of him."

"Who's Amado Fuentes?" Slade asked idly as he continued to study the occupants of the room.

Conklin leaned closer, lowering his voice. "There are folks who say he's Joaquin Murrieta, but that ain't never been proved," he replied. "He owns a *cantina* in The Alley —the Alhambra—biggest and best in that section. He's a sort of leader of the gamblers and other hell-raisers, or so folks say. Ain't nothing ever been proved against him, but plenty suspected. Real high-class Mexican descent, like lots of Californians. Bad medicine in a row. Wouldn't be surprised if he really is tied up with Murrieta or some other scalawags of the same sort. Got a big following, all right, but of the wrong sort.

"By the way," he continued animatedly, "Dave Lang has a standing reward of five-hundred dollars for any of Murrieta's gang brought in. If you'll ride back to the Mohave and pack in those three hellions you downed, reckon there's fifteen-hundred pesos ready and waiting for you."

"It'd be a long hard ride, and I can't say as I have any hankering for that kind of money," Slade smiled reply. "Besides, what proof have you that those claim jumpers belonged to the Murrieta outfit?"

"They said they did."

Slade shook his black head. "Doesn't mean much," he answered. "Brush-popping owlhoots are always claiming to be tied up with some big outfit with a reputation. If every jigger who said he belonged to Curly Bill Brocius's bunch in Arizona had been telling the truth, Curly Bill could have stood up to the United States Army."

"Reckon you're right," replied Conklin, but Slade sensed that his acquiescence was politeness, nothing more. The prospector was convinced that the claim jumpers really were part of the Murrieta outfit. Confound it! maybe he was right!

Not that Slade was especially interested one way or the other. The Murrieta bunch, whoever they might be, posed a problem for the California authorities. His chore was to run down the killers he had trailed across New Mexico and Arizona. That is if they really had continued to California.

Conklin and Trevis began wrangling about the respective worth of quartz versus placer mining. Slade listened to their babble for a while, then finished his drink, told them so long for the moment and left the saloon. He abandoned Main for Aliso Street, sauntered along until he reached The Alley, and turned into the most perfect and full-grown pandemonium he had yet encountered in this gentle City of the Angels.

The crowd from Los Angeles Street to the Plaza was so dense he could hardly squeeze through. Cowboys, ranchers, miners, Indians, Mexicans, Chinese—shouldering from one saloon to another, clinking gold pieces in their palms, bawling, grunting, chattering for action. All appeared obsessed with the one and identical ambition—to get drunk as thoroughly and as quickly as possible.

Slade pushed his way through the swirling throng until he paused in front of a wide, glowing window, across which was lettered in gold: Alhambra. He recalled Trevis or Conklin mentioning that a *cantina* by that name was owned by one Amado Fuentes, Dave Lang's rival for political honors. Moved by curiosity, he passed through the swinging doors and entered.

Fuentes' place was as commodious as the Square Deal and as well furnished, but the lighting was more subdued and it was quieter. Slade liked the atmosphere of the room better than that of Lang's establishment.

However, there was not much difference in the patrons. Perhaps more black velvet and fewer red and plaid shirts, although the mining element was well represented. There were plenty of cowhands drinking or gambling or dancing with the short-skirted bespangled girls. Slade noted that there was a super-abundance of the black-garbed, impassive-faced gentry whose business was to sit at the green-topped tables. Those who were not "working" at the moment drank quietly together at the bar or at tables along the wall and did not appear to mix much with the other patrons of the place. Slade decided that gambling was an important phase of the Alhambra's business.

Passing from table to table, nodding here, dropping a word there, was a man Slade did not need to be told was Amado Fuentes himself.

Amado Fuentes was tall and slender, with the steely slenderness of a finely-tempered rapier blade. He was swarthy of complexion with raven black hair and laughing, reckless brown eyes in the depths of which a twinkle of humor seemed to merge with a glowing light of pure deviltry. He had a firm-lipped, humorous mouth that nevertheless showed evidence of the ability to set tight in merciless ferocity. The mouth, and his high cheek bones, gave hint of a dash of Indian blood leavening the pure Hidalgo strain.

A fighting man who liked to fight for the love of it, Slade diagnosed him. The kind just as willing to have a drink with you or shoot you dead, as the occasion warranted. A first class cavalry leader if a war come along, or a leader of a very different sort of an outfit were there no war handy and his inclinations happened to turn that way. The kind of a bandit leader who goes down in song and story and, after the lapse of a sufficient number of years, is glorified by legend. Robin Hood, Slade felt, must have had just that sort of gay, reckless eyes.

He recalled the old prospector's remark concerning the belief in some quarters that Fuentes and the "resurrected" Joaquin Murrieta might be one and the same. Well, the man's appearance lent some credence to the seemingly absurd suspicion.

Turning to the bar, Slade ordered a drink. In the back-bar mirror he noted Fuentes favoring him with a keen and appraising glance. It was plain the Alhambra owner did not miss a bet; had evidently spotted him the instant he dropped in.

Quite likely Fuentes kept close tab on any newcomer who entered his place of business. Slade suspected he had to, judging from the looks of the crowd. Dynamite in such a gathering, just waiting for somebody to touch off the fuse.

Abruptly Slade had a feeling that other eyes were surveying him intently. He turned casually and met the gaze of the small and elegant leader of the excellent Mexican orchestra, a gaze which mirrored surprise and some other emotion Slade could not at the moment catalogue. Turning back to the bar, he again fixed his gaze on the gleaming back-bar glass. He saw the reflected image of the orchestra leader descend from his low platform and hurry across to where Fuentes was standing. A low-voiced conversation followed. Fuentes again glanced in Slade's direction, turned to the leader and nodded agreement to something the other appeared to be urging. The leader bobbed and smiled, waved the guitar he was holding and hurried toward the bar. In the mirror, Slade watched him come, and turned at the touch on his arm.

The leader bowed low and the smile that touched his lips was one of pure delight.

"*Capitan!*" he said, "Will you not sing for us? It would give us the great pleasure. *Don* Amado requests that you will."

Slade gazed down at the little man and abruptly his cold eyes were very pleasant.

"How do you know I can sing?" he asked.

Again the little Mexican bowed low. "I have heard you sing, *Capitan*, in El Paso, and other places. And who can sing as sings El Halcon, the friend of the lowly?"

Fleetingly, Slade reflected on the futility of endeavoring to escape one's reputation. He hesitated a moment before replying. Oh, what the devil! He'd been spotted as the man of whom a lot of folks, including some puzzled sheriffs and other lawmen, were wont to say—"If he ain't an owlhoot, he misses being one by the skin of his teeth, and tooth skin is mighty thin." So why not sing to please the little Mexican who was regarding him with worshipful eyes?

"With pleasure, *amigo*," he said and followed the musician to the platform.

The leader stepped forward and raised his hand. "Attention, *amigos!*" he called in clear, carrying tones. "I have for you the very great treat; a master of music will play and sing for you."

The babble of talk died to a drone and stilled as expectant faces turned toward the platform. Slade swept his long fingers over the strings of the leader's instrument with crisp power. He played a soft prelude, then flung back his black head and sang—sang one of the plaintive, hauntingly beautiful songs in which the peons, the humble people of Mejico, voice their joys and their sorrows, their wistful yearning for that which they know can never be, their regrets for that which was and is. And as the great metallic baritone-bass pealed and soared under the high ceiling, the dealers forgot to deal, the bartenders forgot to pour drinks, and those whose glasses were filled left them untasted on the bar. The dance-floor girls gathered in little knots, gazing at the tall laughing-eyed singer of dreams as at a bright and glorious vision from a past clouded by the present. Hard faces softened and horny hands were furtively rubbed across eyes that perhaps the smoke had gotten into.

The melody died on a last exquisite note and Slade stood smiling at the roar of applause and the shouts of "Give us another, feller, give us another!"

Slade gave them another—a rollicking old ballad of the range that caused drinkers to hammer the bar and the tables with their glasses, regardless of spilled whiskey, and even the impassive dealers to shuffle their feet in time with the music. Slade played a last booming chord and handed the guitar to the little leader, who bowed until his forehead almost touched the floor.

Abruptly a voice cut through the uproar, a voice thin and high like the rasp of a knife drawn from a rusty scabbard.

"Very, very purty! Now you sing another one just for me, and don't keep me waiting!"

A strange hush fell over the room, in which Slade heard the little orchestra leader's choking whisper, "*Madre de Dios!* Slow Baker!"

TEN

SLADE HAD NOTED the entrance of the man a moment before when he had pushed through the swinging doors and
paused just inside, searching the room with black, dead-
looking eyes, as if in quest of a familiar face. He was a tall
man, tall and thin, with a thinness that was almost skeletal.
His face resembled a death's head, with its cavernous,
deep-set eyes, its sunken cheeks and this gash of mouth
above a long blue chin. His bony hands dangled loosely
at his sides, not far from the black butts of the heavy
guns flaring out from his scrawny hips. His garb was
funereal black, relieved only by the snow of his ruffled
shirt front.

Once in a generation or so there is a man who astounds,
amuses and bewilders other men by the blinding speed
with which he can draw a gun and shoot with utter ac-
curacy at the same time. Add to this talent a lust to kill
and a hatred for all humanity and the result is something
to reckon with. Walt Slade instantly recognized Slow
Baker as that kind of a man; he was familiar with the type.

"Don't care to sing any more right now," he answered
Baker's offensive order.

Slow Baker glared. "Feller," he said, "when I tell a
man to do something, I expect him to do it, fast."

Slade regarded him with eyes that were no longer filled
with laughter. They were the cold gray of a glacier lake
under a cloudy sky, the terrible eyes of El Halcon.

Something in that gaze appeared to give the killer pause.
He hesitated, his own eyes seemed to film, like the lidless
eyes of a snake. Slade's voice suddenly blared at him.

"Get going, you skunk!"

Slow Baker's right hand moved, like the flicker of a
rattlesnake's stroke. Men dived wildly for cover as orange
flashes lanced across the room and the hanging lamps
jumped to the thunder of the reports. Then Walt Slade

lowered his smoking guns and gazed at Slow Baker, who had reeled back, on his corpse-face a look of horrified disbelief. Baker opened his mouth and a torrent of blood gushed forth. He raised himself on tiptoes, screamed a frightful bubbling scream, and plunged forward on his face.

In the dead silence that followed, the little orchestra leader's murmur sounded loud.

"The stroke of The Hawk! Sure as the finger of God!"

Thumbs hooked over the hammers of his cocked guns, Slade glanced warily about. A voice rang out.

"Everybody stay where you are, and keep your hands still. The matter has been taken care of, quite properly."

Slade's eyes glinted sideways toward the bar, from where the voice had come. Amado Fuentes stood at the far end, a cigar in his mouth, which he puffed calmly. The bar itself was quite empty. Behind it stood Fuentes' four drink jugglers, each with a sawed-off shotgun trained on the crowd.

Fuentes spoke again, gesturing toward the body of Slow Baker. "Pack it into the back room and cover it with a blanket," he told a couple of swampers who stood nearby. He turned to the orchestra.

"Music, please!"

The musicians started up a lively tune. The tension broke and talk whirled on all sides. Slade holstered his guns, walked to the bar, paying no attention to the glances turned in his direction, and ordered a drink. He raised the brimming glass with a hand that did not spill a drop and watched Amado Fuentes' approach in the back-bar mirror. He turned to face the saloonkeeper at a touch on his elbow.

"My friend," said Fuentes, "was the man you just killed your enemy?"

"Don't recall ever seeing him before," Slade replied. "Why?"

"Because," said Fuentes, "he came in here to kill you, no doubt as to that."

"Wonder why he did it?" Slade remarked.

"You should be better able to answer that than I," Fuentes countered dryly.

"Not unnatural that you should think so," Slade conceded. He was beginning to have a notion why Baker had made his play.

"Very strange," Fuentes said. "Baker was a notorious killer, and his gun was for hire." He glanced suggestively at Slade, but The Hawk merely nodded.

Fuentes looked a little baffled. He saw that he was getting nowhere.

"Well," he said, "one thing is certain, the community owes you a vote of thanks for ridding it of the pest. Only," he added impressively, "you would do well to be on your guard. There are doubtless those who will seek to avenge Baker's death. Have a drink on the house and enjoy yourself. Here at least you can do so in safety; my men are very much on the lookout for trouble and are well able to handle any situation that may arise."

"Thank you," Slade said. "By the way, can you direct me to the sheriff's office?"

Fuentes seemed slightly taken aback. "Why—why it is right over on Spring Street; just a few minutes' walk from here. The sheriff's name is Branch Harding."

"Thank you," Slade said again. He set his empty glass on the bar, nodded to the saloonkeeper and walked out.

As soon as the swinging doors had closed on his back, a storm of comment arose.

"I saw it but I don't believe it," declared an old cowhand. "Downed Slow Baker! Shot him to pieces! Slow never had a chance. *Slow* Baker was right! That big jigger made him look slow as a snail climbing a slick log. Slow finally ran up against a man he couldn't make mad enough to reach and then kill him in 'self defense.'"

"What I'd like to know," said another, "is who the devil he is?"

"Me, too," said the first speaker.

Felipe, the little orchestra leader could have told them, but didn't. He did tell Amado Fuentes when the owner questioned him.

"He is a strange man, *patron*. Where there is trouble, or sorrow, or injustice, or wrong, he appears. From where, none knows. And when he departs he leaves behind him peace and content. A strange man! There are some who say, and they are evil, that he is *El Diablo* himself."

"As to that I couldn't say," replied Fuentes. "But I agree with you that he is a strange man, and most unusual.

I never saw such eyes! They seem to look right inside of you!"

"And if there are dark places one would rather not be seen, then—beware!" Felipe said gravely. "*Patron*, well may Joaquin Murrieta now beware."

"What do you mean by that?" Fuentes asked sharply, giving him a keen look.

"I mean," said Felipe, "that Joaquin Murrieta is an evil man, and El Halcon does not like evil men."

Fuentes regarded him thoughtfully. "Again you may be right," he conceded. "Yes, I think it behooves Murrieta to walk warily, to walk warily."

He turned and strode back to the bar. Felipe followed him with his eyes and stroked his little black mustache.

"Ha! *patron*," he murmured inaudibly, "I believe I have given you food for thought."

Slade located the sheriff's office in the front of a solidly constructed building that was evidently the county jail. A light burned behind the window so he knocked on the closed door. In answer to a grumpy "Come in!" he opened the door and entered.

Sheriff Branch Harding was old and lean and lanky. He had a tight mouth beneath a drooping mustache and frosty blue eyes. He waved his visitor to a chair and eyed him keenly. However, his voice was pleasant enough.

"What can I do for you, son?"

"I wish to report, sir, that I just killed a man," Slade replied.

"That so?" said the sheriff, who didn't appear shocked or overly impressed. "Nothing unusual about that in this blasted town. Why did you kill him?"

"He reached."

"Humph!" said the sheriff. "Had you been having trouble with him?"

"Never saw him before he stepped into the Alhambra," Slade replied. "He evidently came looking for a fight, spotted me first off and jumped me."

"The Alhambra!" growled the sheriff. "Always some trouble busting loose in that rumhole. Some day I'll bar the doors. And he reached first?"

"He did."

"Happen to catch his name?"

"Baker, somebody said."

The sheriff sat bolt upright in his chair. "You don't mean Slow Baker?" he asked.

"I believe that was what somebody called him," Slade answered.

"And he wasn't asleep or drunk or something?"

"Certainly wasn't asleep and appeared to be cold sober."

The sheriff leaned forward and fixed Slade with a gimlet gaze.

"You trying to tell me that Slow Baker reached first and you outdrew him and killed him?" he demanded.

"No, I'm not trying to tell you, I'm telling you."

Sheriff Harding tugged his mustache and swore; his gaze was still incredulous.

"Slow Baker," he said, spacing his words, "Slow Baker is—was—reputed to have the fastest and most accurate gun hand in California."

"I'm not from California," Slade answered, the ghost of a grin tugging at the corners of his mouth.

The sheriff swore some more. "Where the devil are you from?" he demanded.

"Texas."

"Maybe that explains it," grunted Harding. "You're a long ways from home."

"I've been farther."

"And why was you run out of Texas?"

"Wasn't run out."

Sheriff Harding decided he was getting exactly nowhere with his interrogation. Abruptly he smiled, and his lined old face was suddenly very pleasant.

"Son," he said, "you'll have to pass over me being sort of skeptical, but a man who can pull faster than Slow Baker isn't run into every day. Suppose you tell me just what happened, and everything that led up to what happened. This may turn out, for you, at least, something more serious than downing an ornery gunslinger and doing decent citizens a favor. I want all the details so I can advise you."

Slade told him. The sheriff tugged his mustache and looked very thoughtful.

"Son," he said, "here comes the advice, the kind of advice perhaps a law enforcement officer shouldn't give, but I figure the circumstances are a mite out of the ordinary. You own a horse?"

Slade nodded, his grin widening. He anticipated what was coming.

"The advice," said the sheriff, "is for you to fork that horse and ride, and keep on riding; all the way back to Texas might be a good notion. Slow Baker didn't come gunning for you on his own account. Very seldom did he shoot somebody without getting paid—in advance—for doing so. Somehow you've antagonized a mighty bad bunch, just who I don't know for sure. They're out to get you, and they will get you if you hang around the section. So ride!"

"Horse is a mite tired after a long ride across the Mohave," Slade replied.

Sheriff Harding had no difficulty understanding that his well meant word of advice was rejected.

"Okay," he said, "it's your funeral. And that's just what it will very likely be, your *funeral*. Drop around here tomorrow at ten, if you're still alive. I suppose we'll have to hold an inquest on the reptile. Somebody to testify Baker reached first?"

"I suppose a hundred or so people could do so," Slade answered. "Including the owner of the place. Amado Fuentes, I believe he is called."

"Fuentes will be enough," grunted the sheriff. "No matter what else he may be, he's no liar. And so old Slow at last didn't get a chance to plead 'self defense.' Be seeing you, son, if you're still alive."

"I aim to be," Slade smiled as he stood up, towering over the sheriff, himself a six-footer. "And thank you for everything, sir."

Outside, Slade headed for the stable where he proposed to sleep, his thoughts on recent events rather than his immediate surroundings. Began to look like Trevis and Conklin were right, he thought. The three claim jumpers had belonged to the Murrieta outfit, or some outfit of a similar nature, presumably with headquarters in Los Angeles. Drunk and talkative, the old fellows had sounded off to all and sundry concerning the shooting in the canyon.

Attempted retaliation had been swift, and staged in a spectacular manner that would have left an impression on all who saw or heard about it, and it wouldn't have taken people long to understand why he was killed. The tried and tested method of organized outlawry—rule by terror. Slow Baker had been the executioner for the band. Well, the attempt had failed. Nothing to do now but watch out for the next one. He wasn't going anywhere until he picked up a clue to the killers he was trailing. With a shrug, he turned down the quiet side street toward the stable. Suddenly the silence was shattered by a frightful scream instantly echoed by a high-pitched rasping shriek of agony and terror.

ELEVEN

SLADE BOUNDED FORWARD. He recognized that first awful sound as the scream of a maddened horse, and he knew what horse. He had heard Shadow scream that way before. He reached the stable door and thrust the key into the lock.

From inside the stable came another sound, a sound dull and muffled but continuous, a thudding and thrashing about, and Shadow's loud and hideous whinnying rising above whimpering cries quickly stifled.

"Hold it, Shadow! Hold it!" he shouted in an agony of apprehension.

The key fitted illy and precious seconds were lost before Slade tore open the door and rushed into the stable. Upstairs he could hear the patter of the stable-keeper's bare feet on the floor.

A beam of light filtered down the stairs from a bracket lamp in the hall above to show, rising from the gloom of the first stall, a fiendish black head with ears laid back, eyes rolling, and teeth laid bare—teeth whose gleaming white were horribly blotched, in whose vigorous grip something dangled.

Vergara, the keeper, came racing down the stairs, his big knife in one hand, a gun in the other.

"What in blazes is going on?" he yelled. He stopped, staring at the stall. "What's he got in his mouth?"

"Looks like part of a shirt," Slade replied as he moved forward.

"Blood of ten thousand devils! What's that over there?" Vergara pointed to a corner of the stall, where something lay sprawled and twisted and contorted, hideously battered and torn and trampled, something which lay very still.

Slade led Shadow from the blood-splattered stall and stroked his quivering neck with a soothing hand. Only then did he speak.

66

"That," he said grimly, "was a man!"

Vergara swore. "Did he try to steal the horse?"

"Perhaps," Slade replied. "Wonder how'd he get in? The door was locked when I got here."

Vergara gestured to a little glassless window that opened onto the stall from the outside wall.

"A small man could have come in by way of that," he said. "Let's see."

He entered the stall, gripped a flaccid arm and hauled the broken body into the light.

The man, or what was left of him, was short and scrawny. He had a thin weasel-face now stamped with a look of unutterable horror. At his hip swung a heavy gun, and there was a long knife in his belt.

"Well heeled," muttered Vergara. He stared at the corpse, turned and gave Slade a curious glance. "You're sure the door was locked when you came in? Yes? He couldn't open it from the inside without a key, so he must have planned to go the way he came. And he certainly couldn't have taken a horse through the window, and there's nothing else here to steal."

"So," Slade prompted.

"So," Vergara said dryly, "it would seem that one of us has an enemy. Oh, he came in here with the notion of killing someone, all right. No doubt as to that."

"I wouldn't argue it," Slade answered. "Yes, he had something like that in mind, I'd say. Guess when he slid through the window he touched the horse, which naturally jumped and snorted. Then, the chances are, he grabbed for its nose to keep it quiet; and that was enough for Shadow, who allows no stranger to put a hand on him."

"Good horse!" grunted Vergara. "Well, guess the sheriff had better be notified; he'll want to look things over. I'll take care of that, if you'll stick around till I get back."

"I'll be here."

Verega hurried upstairs, donned his boots and slipped out the door, glancing keenly to right and left. Slade watched him turn the corner, closed the door and rolled a cigarette. He had almost finished the cigarette when Vergara returned with the sheriff.

The old peace officer glanced at the corpse and turned to Slade.

"See what I meant?" he remarked significantly.

"Looks like you might have the right slant on things," Slade conceded.

"Got a spare horse blanket, Vergara?" the sheriff asked. "I'll round up a couple of swampers and we'll pack the varmint over to the coroner's office and lay him out beside that other reptile. Doc Cooper's acquiring quite a collection since you hit town, son. Looks like the beginning of a good poker hand—two of a kind, so far. Try and not break the sequence by being the odd card. By the way, I don't believe I caught your name."

Slade supplied it. The sheriff gave him a peculiar look. "Slade," he repeated meditatively. "Hmmm! Slade. Well, be at the inquest at ten tomorrow, if you're still alive. What do you aim to do now?"

"I'm going to give my horse a good rubdown and then go to bed."

"A good notion," said the sheriff. "I'll go get those swampers."

Slade did go to bed and slept soundly. He was at the sheriff's office at ten o'clock.

The inquest was brief. Without taking the trouble to leave the box, the jury brought in a verdict that was typically cow country in its pithy terseness. It " 'lowed" that Slow Baker got exactly what had been coming to him for a long time and commended Slade for ridding the community of a dangerous element and expressed the hope that he'd stick around long enough to line sights with some more of the same sort. It also stated that Shadow rated an extra helping of oats for cashing in a horse thief.

As the jury and the spectators filed out, Sheriff Harding motioned to Slade to remain. When they were alone, he closed the door, sat down at his desk and proceeded to fill his pipe with great deliberation. For some moments he regarded The Hawk in silence, then,

"Been hearing some stories about you."

"Yes?"

"Yes, among others that you're just about the smartest owlhoot that ever growed in Texas."

"That's covering a lot of territory." Slade smiled.

"I agree," said the sheriff. "Texas has turned out some prime specimens. Incidentally, we've got enough of the home-grown variety without importing any."

"I'm inclined to agree with you there," Slade replied.

The sheriff looked a trifle exasperated. He puffed vigorously on his pipe.

"Slade," he said abruptly, "why are you here?"

El Halcon rolled and lighted a cigarette before replying, his eyes never leaving the old peace officer's face. He liked what he saw there and decided to do a little talking. Briefly, he related what happened in the valley east of El Paso. The sheriff nodded.

"So you're riding the vengeance trail, eh?" he observed.

"In a way," Slade conceded.

Sheriff Harding shook his head. "A bad trail to follow," he said. "Feller riding it can mighty easy find himself on the wrong side of the law."

"Again I'm ready to agree with you," Slade replied.

"But you still figure to try and run down those hellions."

"I do."

Sheriff Harding nodded thoughtfully. "Well, there's nothing much I can do until and if you violate the law."

"I'll try not to, sir," Slade promised.

"Make sure you succeed," warned the sheriff. "Well, I've got work to do. Suppose you'll be hanging around the Square Deal or the Alhambra tonight?"

"I wouldn't be surprised."

"Okay, the chances are I'll see you in one or the other." Harding turned to the papers on his desk to show the interview was ended. Slade rose and started for the door. As he reached it, Harding spoke without looking up from his papers.

"Been to Tombstone, Arizona, haven't you?"

"I have," Slade replied. His hand on the knob, he shot Harding a curious glance.

"A feller, an old friend of mine, who came down from Nevada a little while back to investigate some mining properties he's interested in, and who spent considerable time in Tombstone, got to talking about a feller he met there named Slade. Talked quite a bit."

"That so?" Slade said. "What was his name?"

Sheriff Harding looked up, and there was a trace of amusement in his frosty eyes when he replied.

"His name was, and is—Wyatt Earp. Good day, Mr. Slade."

Slade stared at him, opened the door and departed

closing it behind him. Outside he halted, gazing at the closed door. Not often was Ranger Walt Slade caught off balance; but right now he felt a mite flabbergasted.

"Just how much does that old coot know?" he asked the brass doorknob. The doorknob was not responsive. Slade walked on, thinking.

He had met the famous frontier marshal, Wyatt Earp, in Tombstone and had been able to do him a favor—saving Earp's life, in fact. Wyatt Earp knew him as El Halcon. As to whether he also knew he was a Texas Ranger, Slade was not sure, although he rather thought Wyatt suspected he was. Perhaps, however, he didn't, so Slade wondered just what he had told Sheriff Harding. It might well have a decided bearing on his activities in California.

Shortly before the death of his father, following business reverses suffered by the elder Slade, Walt Slade had graduated from a famous college of engineering. The post-graduate course he had planned to take became impossible for the time being, so when Captain McNelty suggested he come into the Rangers and continue his studies in spare time, young Walt thought the notion a good one. It did not take him too long to get more from private study than he could have hoped for from the postgrad but, meanwhile, Ranger work had gotten a strong hold on him. He was still young, plenty of time to be an engineer; he'd stick with the Rangers for a while.

In the course of his Ranger activities, due to his habit of working undercover when possible and often not revealing his Ranger connections, Slade had built up a dual reputation. People who knew him to be a Ranger held him in high esteem. "The most capable and most fearless Ranger of them all," many said. Plenty who didn't know it vigorously maintained that El Halcon was just a shrewd and dangerous outlaw too smart to get caught. Slade did nothing to remedy the state of affairs, having found the dubious honor, while laying him open to considerable personal danger, often worked to his advantage, providing sources of information that would have been closed to a known law-enforcement officer.

Right now he wondered if Sheriff Branch Harding's knowing him as El Halcon would be good or bad.

Slade spent the remainder of the day moving about the

bustling town. Its turbulent activity never ceased and there was a spirit of optimism abroad and an enthusiasm nothing could quench. He quickly decided that the old prospector was right when he predicted Los Angeles would some day be a big city. The location was a natural and there was plenty of space to spread out, with deep waterports almost in the town's front yard. He studied faces, listened to conversations. Several times he heard mention of Joaquin Murrieta and his activities—the bandit leader was a prime topic of conversation in all the saloons. Slade's encounter with Slow Baker had revivified interest in Murrieta and it was freely predicted that the outlaw would cut loose somewhere else before long.

But nowhere did he learn anything to cause him to believe the Murrieta outfit was one and the same, or connected with, the killers he trailed from Texas. Nor did he unearth any clue as to who they might be or their whereabouts. Perhaps he had been wrong in heading for California instead of giving the Arizona wilds a more careful once-over.

"But darn it, I still believe they kept heading west," he told Shadow when he returned to the stable shortly after dark.

Removing his boots, he lay down on the bed and was almost instantly sound asleep. He awoke with a start, glanced at his watch and chuckled as he realized it was nearly midnight. Evidently the recent hectic excitement had tired him more than he realized. He descended the stairs, sluiced in the icy waters of the trough and headed for something to eat. He decided on the Alhambra rather than the Square Deal, where very likely the two old prospectors would be raising merry blazes.

The food served by the Alhambra was excellent and Slade enjoyed his meal. He saw Amada Fuentes moving about, spending a little time at various tables and keeping a close watch on the games and the behavior on the dance floor. Fuentes nodded pleasantly, but did not approach. Felipe, the orchestra leader, bowed deeply to El Halcon.

Slade was sipping a final cup of coffee when Sheriff Harding entered and crossed to his table. Slade waved him to a vacant chair and called a waiter.

"Yes, I'll have a drink," said the sheriff. "No, nothing else, I just ate."

"So, you're still alive," he observed to Slade after the waiter had departed.

"So I'm led to believe," Slade smiled reply.

"And nothing else has happened?"

"Not so far," Slade answered.

"Well, something will, you can bet on that," the sheriff growled morosely. "If not to you, to somebody else. No peace in this section of late."

TWELVE

Sheriff Harding proved not only a true prophet but a timely one. He had barely emptied his glass and motioned for a refill when the swinging doors crashed open and a wild-eyed man rushed in.

"Where's the sheriff?" he yelled. "They said he was here!"

"This way, Wilkins," called Harding. "What's the matter with you?"

The man darted across the room to the table.

"Blake and Carnes, my partners, my partners!" he bawled. "Robbed, shot, killed, murdered!"

"Get a hold of yourself, feller!" roared the sheriff. "What in blazes are you talking about?"

"I told you!" shrieked Wilkins. "They're both dead!"

Slade reached out, gripped the near-hysterical man by the arm and gently but firmly eased him into a chair and motioned a waiter to bring him a drink.

"Now tell us just what happened," he said.

His quiet voice and steady eyes exerted a calming influence on Wilkins. He still breathed in gulps but he relaxed in the chair, seized the glass the hurrying waiter brought and drained it at a swallow. He wiped his lips with a trembling hand and addressed himself to Slade rather than to the sputtering sheriff.

"At our claim, up in White Horse Canyon, we been doing mighty well—had a fat poke of dust and nuggets. My mule had strayed up the canyon and I went looking for her, for we'd figured tomorrow to come to town to stow away our gold and have a bust. I found the critter and headed back to the camp. Was maybe half a mile off when I heard the shooting, a devil of a lot of shooting. Thought it was funny—nothing around there for the boys to be shooting at. I come to the edge of the brush

73

and stopped where I could see the camp. I saw them haul out the pokes of dust and stow 'em in the saddle pouches of some horses standing a little ways off. Then they built up the fire and went to work on our supply of chuck. I had to stay right where I was 'cause I'd have had an open space to cross to get by the camp. Had left my rifle at camp when I went to look for the mule. Just had to keep undercover and wait till dark. They got rigs off their horses and cooked and ate. Was beginning to get dark. They built up the fire some more and spread blankets. I guessed they figured to spend the night at the camp. It got darker and I sneaked past, got on the mule and headed for town."

"Seven or eight in the bunch, I believe you said," Slade commented, motioning to the waiter to bring another drink.

"That's right."

"And you think they planned to camp there for the night?"

"That's what I figure," nodded Wilkins, gulping his drink.

"Wouldn't they know there were three men working the claim and be on the lookout for you?" Slade asked.

"Don't see any reason why they'd know that," replied Wilkins. "Wasn't but two mules and a couple of pack burros tethered at the camp, which made it look like there was only two fellers working there."

The crowd had packed about the table and was hanging on every word that was said.

"The Murrieta bunch, sure as blazes!" Slade heard the mutter.

"Right!" agreed another voice. "They're always going for miners with fat pokes, when they ain't robbing banks or stage coaches."

Slade glanced at the sheriff. "How far to White Horse Canyon?"

"I should be able to make it there with a bunch by daybreak," the sheriff replied.

"You'd better get moving," Slade said.

"You're right," agreed the sheriff. "I'll get my three deputies and pick out a couple more fellers." He stood up and headed for the door, the crowd parting to make way. Slade paced beside him.

"I'd like to go along," he said when they were outside and away from the crowd.

"Guess I can take a chance on you," grunted Harding. "I'll swear you in as a special deputy and give you a badge. Come along to the office, one of the boys will be there and I'll send him to round up the others. Better get your horse right away."

Rounding up the deputies and the specials took longer than expected and fully three-quarters of an hour elapsed before the posse finally got under way.

"I believe those fellers in the Alhambra were right and it is the Murrieta bunch, or some of them," observed the sheriff as they rode north. "If we can hit them at daybreak when they're just stirring we should be able to bag the lot. And this time," he added, "I want some prisoners if possible. There's always a chance of making somebody talk and maybe we can find out who the devil this ghost-man Murrieta is. No doubt about it, there's a regular outlaw organization in this section, been building up for a long time, and if we can just learn who's the brains back of it, bustin' it up will be easy. What do you think, Slade?"

"Squash the head of the snake and you don't have to worry about the rest of it," Slade replied.

The night was overcast and dark, the trail rough and broken. Walt Slade rode silent and thoughtful. To get away from the mutter of talk, he dropped back to the rear of the posse. Another rider slowed back beside him. Sheriff Harding.

"What do you think, son?" the sheriff asked in low tones.

"I think," Slade replied quietly, "that you had better take every precaution and be very much on the alert."

"Why?" asked the sheriff, his voice a trifle startled.

"Because," Slade explained, "part of Wilkins' story didn't ring true to me."

"The devil!" exclaimed the sheriff. "I've known Tad Wilkins for years. He's an honest old coot and couldn't tell anything but the truth."

"The truth as he sees it," Slade countered.

"And what do you mean by that? And what part of his yarn are you thinking about?"

Slade ignored the first question. The second, he answered with an explanation.

"The part in which he believed the outlaws would not know there were three men working the claim. If they are as smart as they've continually shown evidence of being, they would have known very well three men were working there. They would see only two mules, as Wilkins said, but they would, in my opinion, reason correctly that the third man was up the canyon somewhere trying to drop a loop on the third mule, which had strayed. So why weren't some of them spread out in the brush waiting to mow him down as soon as he showed?"

"Why?" asked the sheriff.

Slade glanced ahead before replying. He could just make out the forms of the other riders and knew they were too far away to overhear the low-voiced conversation between him and the sheriff.

"Because they figured he'd slip by them in the dark and carry the story of what happened to you in town, which was just what they wanted him to do."

"But why would they want him to do that?" demanded the sheriff.

"Because they'd know you would immediately head for the canyon, hoping to come up with them before they moved on."

"You've still got me plumb puzzled," said Harding. "All I seem to say is 'why'?"

Slade chuckled under his breath, although he was in no mood for mirth.

"Owlhoots," he replied, "have no use for an honest law enforcement officer. I understand there's an election coming up soon. With you out of the way it might be possible for organized outlawry such as you seem to have here in Los Angeles County to slide in a man not too unfriendly toward them and, to put it mildly, not exactly alert when it comes to running them down. It's been done before. You may recall a recent classic example in Cochise County, Arizona."

"You're right about that," growled the sheriff. "A certain gent holding office there sure wasn't much on the prod against Curly Bill and his bunch. Blast it! you've got me worried. After all, I was just a range boss before I got mixed up in the infernal sheriffin' business. I can't think things out that way."

"Hardly adequate training to fit one to cope with such an outfit as appears to be working in this section," Slade conceded. "But if you don't mind taking a little advice from a 'notorious owlhoot,' we may be able to tangle those gents' twine for them."

" 'Notorious owlhoot,' the devil!" snorted the sheriff. "No matter, anyhow, I'll be only too glad of help from somebody who knows what he's talking about. You're in charge from now on. I'll follow your lead."

"We won't make it obvious," Slade said. "Just back me up in what I may suggest."

"You're darn right I will," replied Harding.

"Come on, let's get in front," Slade said. "How much farther to the canyon? It'll be daylight before long."

"We should make it by then at the outside," predicted Harding. "Then it's just a hop and a skip to where those poor old coots had their claim."

Nearly an hour had passed and the sky was graying when the sheriff announced they were nearing the canyon.

"Single file and hug the cliff," Slade told him. "Slow up a bit, too, and keep your ears open."

Another fifteen minutes and the mouth of the canyon came into view, dimly seen in the slowly strengthening light. It was brush-choked and a single narrow trail wormed through the tangled growth. Slade spoke to the sheriff, who held up his hand; the posse jolted to a halt, glancing questioningly at their leader.

"Hold them here till I give things a once-over," Slade said. "Go barging in there and we're taking a chance of getting blown from under our hats."

He dismounted and went forward on foot.

"That big hellion moves like an Injun," a posse member muttered to Harding. "One second you see him, the next you don't. Where the devil did he get to?"

"Slid into the brush," replied the sheriff. "Makes no more noise than a snake in a cactus patch. Take it easy till he gets back."

Slade was gone a full ten minutes. He appeared unexpectedly to the left of the posse, looming tall and lithe in the deceptive light.

"Now how'd he get there without us seeing him?" somebody wondered.

Sheriff Harding leaned forward in his saddle. "What'd you find out?" he asked eagerly.

"Among other things, that they haven't come down the canyon," Slade answered.

"Then they're still up there?"

"Not necessarily," Slade replied.

"What makes you say that?" demanded Harding. "And what makes you sure they didn't come out this way?"

"No horses have come down the canyon since last night, no marks of any," Slade said. "Tracks of one mule, coming fast. And tracks of one horse, going fast—up canyon."

"And what the devil does that mean?" demanded the bewildered peace officer.

"I'd say," Slade answered dryly, "that it means somebody rode out of town and headed north before we did."

Sheriff Harding swore a blistering oath. "To warn the devils we were coming so they could skallyhoot out the other end of this crack, eh?"

"Possibly," Slade conceded. "At least to tell them we were coming, how many of us there would be, and when we could be expected to get here."

Branch Harding, while not being exactly a brilliant peace officer, was far from stupid.

"I think I get it," he said slowly. "They expect us to ride up to the camp looking to find them all asleep. Instead, they'll be all set to mow us down. Is that right?"

"Not exactly," Slade answered. "I think we can ride to the camp in perfect safety, although we will take precautions against the possibility of my being mistaken. All set to go?"

He headed Shadow toward the trail through the brush, leaving the others to follow, which they did, albeit with a certain reluctance and plenty of evidence of nervousness.

It was ticklish business, threading their way between the walls of encroaching brush, not knowing from one minute to the next whether a blast of gunfire would roar from the silent chaparral. Slade rode several paces in front, lounging easily in his saddle.

"Say, I smell smoke," one of the deputies suddenly muttered.

"Yes," Slade replied without turning his head, "the smoke of a fire that has burned down almost to ashes."

Slade reined in. "This will be far enough till I have a look at things," he said. Again he dismounted and glided forward, vanishing from his companions' sight. Hands close to their gun butts, the posse waited, the minutes dragging slowly, the light steadily increasing.

Again El Halcon materialized, apparently from nowhere. "Everything okay," he said as he swung into the saddle, not taking the trouble to lower his voice. "They've been gone better than an hour, I'd say. Come on."

Full daylight had broken when they reached the camp. Two mules and a couple of burros grazed contentedly, pricking their ears at the new arrivals, then returning their attention to their morning meal. The camp effects were scattered about and not far from the ashes of the fire the bodies of the two murdered prospectors lay sprawled on the ground. The posse members swore bitterly as they gazed on the pitiful remains and then began poking around the camp which had been set up near a small spring of clear water.

"Hey!" one called. "Here's their tracks, leading up the canyon."

Sheriff Harding hurried to the speaker. "He's right," he called to Slade. "They're heading up the canyon."

"Yes, leading up the canyon," Slade agreed and began manufacturing a cigarette with the slim fingers of his left hand. "Where else did you expect them to go?"

"Why—why no place, I reckon," the sheriff replied.

"But hadn't we better hightail after them?" asked one of the deputies. "We'll have to hustle to catch 'em up before they get out the other end. Canyon's only about eight miles long."

The sheriff glanced at Slade, who lighted his cigarette and took a deep drag.

"I'd say there's no hurry," he said. "If they really sifted sand leaving here, with more than an hour's start they'll get in the clear—if there's someplace to get in the clear the other side of this hole."

"Plenty of places," said the sheriff.

Slade had arrived at a definite conclusion about the outlaws' actions. If he was right, he believed he might be able to turn the tables on a smart and utterly ruthless band of law-breakers and killers.

"Then, Sheriff, I suggest we take it easy up the canyon and keep our eyes open," he said.

Sheriff Harding stared at him, opened his lips to ask another question, then closed them.

"Okay," he said, "we'll do just that. Let's go."

The posse got under way, riding at a steady pace with Slade slightly in the lead. With nothing happening, they covered nearly three miles, the trail constantly ascending. The canyon broadened considerably, scored by dips and ridges, and the growth thinned somewhat, but was still thick enough to provide cover.

There was little talk. The deputies and specials were nervous and ill-at-ease. From time to time they glanced somewhat askance at Slade, and at the imperturbable sheriff, who apparently had not a care in the world.

Slade himself was constantly studying the terrain ahead. Abruptly he slowed Shadow's gait and a moment later pulled the big horse to a halt. The posse jostled to a standstill behind him.

"See something?" Sheriff Harding asked.

"Yes," Slade replied. "Look at those crows up top the next sag."

Harding squinted his eyes at the dipping and circling black dots above a bristle of growth which topped the distant rise.

"Seem put out about something," he remarked.

"Could be only a rattlesnake sunning himself on a rock, or a mountain lion stretched out on a limb," Slade observed.

"Who cares about a lot of squawkin' crows!" exclaimed one of the specials, a young cowhand with an impetuous look. "Let's get going before those hellions give us the slip. Ain't no sense in dawdlin' along this way."

Slade turned in the saddle and let his steady gray eyes rest on the puncher's face.

"I think it would be a good notion to let the crows monopolize the squawking," he commented.

The cowboy started to bristle but apparently thought better of it and subsided to under-the-breath mutterings.

"Those crows are acting as they always do when something they're afraid of or unfamiliar with is near their nests," Slade said. "It's not likely to be a snake—they'd be going for him instead of flying high. And they usually pay very little attention to a lion, with which they are familiar and which never bothers them. Somewhere in that growth is something that is strange to them and which they consider to be dangerous."

"You mean it might be those hellions holed up waiting for us?" asked Harding.

"Not impossible," Slade replied. He studied the terrain ahead for a moment. "If they are up there, they wouldn't have been able to spot us yet, because of the growth," he said. "In fact, I figure we'd be within a couple of hundred yards of that thicket before they could see us; but that would be plenty soon enough for them if they happen to be holed up in the brush."

"And a bit too soon for us," growled the sheriff. Slade nodded.

"If they are holed up there, they'd be right under the side wall of the canyon," he observed reflectively. "You'll notice the side wall from here on isn't too steep for a man to scramble up it, and it's all brush-grown. I believe I can slip up there and get in behind them. I'd be higher than they are and, the chances are, will be able to see them without them seeing me. If they are there, we can possibly figure some way to give them a surprise. I'll have a try at it."

"You'll be taking one devil of a chance, son," the sheriff protested. "Maybe it would be better if we all slid up there. Then the odds would be more even if something goes wrong."

Slade vetoed the suggestion. "They'd be sure to hear a body of men coming and be ready for us," he said. "One man makes less noise than a number. I'm pretty sure I can sneak up there alone without being heard."

"Well, all right," Harding agreed reluctantly. "We'll hole up here and wait, but you be careful."

The posse dismounted and tethered their horses in the growth that clothed the sloping wall of the canyon. Then they squatted beneath bushes and rolled cigarettes, knowing that the wisps of smoke could not be seen from the distant rise. Slade hitched his cartridge belts a little higher and slid noiselessly into the chaparral. The others settled down to a nervous wait, filled with all sorts of unpleasant apprehensions.

It was the young cowhand who broke the silence that had settled like a pall over the group.

"Sheriff," he said, "I'm scared we're taking one devil of a chance. Suppose that jigger is in cahoots with the bunch we're trailing and has gone to let them know just where we are? We'd be settin' quail. And I've heard folks say he's an owlhoot himself, a mighty smart one."

"He could be," the sheriff conceded cheerfuly.

"Then we are taking a chance," insisted the cowboy.

Sheriff Harding pinched out his cigarette with a grimace of distaste and hauled out his old black pipe. Stuffing it with tobacco, he peered over the bowl at the cowboy.

"Well, if you feel that way about it, Grumley, maybe you'd better turn tail and scoot back down the canyon where you'll be safe," he remarked, touching a match to the pipe.

Grumley's face turned scarlet. He glared at the sheriff, started to speak, then grinned.

"Guess I asked for it," he said. "I ain't scootin' no-where, and I reckon you know what you're doing."

"I reckon I do," said the sheriff, puffing vigorously.

THIRTEEN

SLADE MADE HIS WAY rapidly but silently toward the rise, going diagonally up the side slope. A couple of hundred yards from where the crows swooped and circled, he slowed down.

It took him more than a quarter of an hour to cover the last hundred yards. When he was in a position he judged to be directly above the crest, he wormed his way carefully down the slope. Overhead the crows, unseen through the thick canopy of leaves and branches, cawed querulously. Slade crawled on. He had drifted down the slope as noiselessly as a hunting wolf when he spied movement in the scattered brush that overlooked the trail. He halted instantly. A moment later he made out the figure of a man crouching behind a boulder. Nearby was another. A bristle of mesquite sheltered a third. The outlaws! All set and waiting for the posse to appear.

Recalling the number named by Wilkins, the prospector, Slade reasoned there should be four or five more somewhere around. Intent on discovering their whereabouts, he took a cautious step forward, planting his foot softly on what to all appearances was firm ground.

It wasn't. It was the mouth of an abandoned badger hole, filled and drifted over by falling leaves.

Down he plunged, lost his balance and fell heavily with a prodigious crackling and smashing of twigs and branches.

The crouching figures whirled, leaped erect, glaring in the direction of the sound. Slade had barely time to free his leg from the hole and roll behind an outcropping of stone before guns cracked in the growth below and bullets chipped branches and fluttered leaves all about him.

Crouching, he slid his guns from their sheaths and waited. From below came the sound of voices, then the scrape and shuffle of boots moving in his direction. Peering cautiously over the ragged lip of stone, he caught glimpses of figures crawling up the slope. He fired three shots, and ducked back as answering bullets thudded against the stone. From below came a howl of pain and a wild thrashing about. Evidently one of the slugs had found a mark.

Which was all to the good, but he was outnumbered seven or eight to one and in the thick brush the outlaws would fan out and surround him.

Abruptly silence fell, which Slade did not like at all. He thrust a gun muzzle over the top of the rock and sprayed the brush with slugs. A yell echoed the reports and a torrent of curses.

A bullet whined past, cutting diagonally across his shelter. Another whistled from the opposite direction. The outlaws couldn't see him yet, but they were crawling through the brush on either side to outflank him. Once let them get above where he crouched and he'd be exposed to a deadly crossfire.

He craned his neck trying to spot some nearby nook or crevice in which he could hole up. The only thing which looked at all hopeful was a rift in a ledge that wormed up the sag a score of paces distant. If he could get into that and be protected on three sides, he might be able to stand off the attack. But to cross the fairly open space to reach it appeared a convenient way to commit suicide. And if he didn't make the attempt, the ultimate result would very likely be the same.

Searching the growth on either side, he groped about until his hand encountered a loose fragment of stone. He scooped it from its bed beneath the leaves and with an underhand motion pitched it down the slope and a little to the right. It struck the ground with a thump and rustle.

Instantly the unseen guns boomed. Lead screeched through the air in the direction of the rolling stone.

"There he goes!" bellowed a voice. "After him!"

Slade bounded from behind the ledge and raced across the open to the crevice. As he reached it, a wild yell went up. He dived head first into the crack, a bullet whipping through the space he'd occupied a split second before. Scrambling to his feet, he writhed about and backed into the narrowing crevice until he could go no farther.

With a swift glance he took in the situation. The floor of the crevice dipped down sharply and from where he crouched, little more than his head would provide a target for a man coming straight at the opening. And he was protected by stone walls on either side and to the rear.

But there was one method of approach that had to be reckoned with. Very likely somebody would quickly realize that it would be possible to creep up to the edge of the crack and peer around into its depths.

A shadow moved in the brush directly in front of the opening. He snapped a shot at it and was rewarded by a wailing curse and the crash of a body. The growth was quiet after that and strain his ears as he would, he could detect no sound of the outlaws approaching his shelter. Perhaps they had decided that smoking him out would be too costly.

Slade didn't think so, however. He waited.

Had the outlaw crept forward from the west instead of from the east, he would very likely have accomplished his purpose. His shadow cast by the morning sun saved the Ranger. Slade hurled himself sideways and down as the shadow fell across the floor of the crevice. A gun roared thunderously between the close walls of stone and the bullet ripped through the sleeve of his shirt. Flat on his back, he fired upward at the head of a man peering over the edge of the fissure.

The head jerked back. Its owner slid over the lip of the crevice and thudded to the ground directly in front of Slade, a blue hole squarely between his fixed and staring eyes.

Slade turned over on his side, watching the front opening and the ragged edges above. Outside, voices were calling back and forth, but he could not understand what was said. The voices stopped and the silence which followed was singularly disquieting.

Again a shadow fell across the fissure, but this time it was not cast by a man's head. It was the shadow of a heavy boulder that hurtled downward and crashed on the floor near the entrance.

The first stone was followed by another and still another which slammed from side to side of the narrow slit, raising a cloud of dust that half blinded the Ranger. He blinked the dust from his eyes and edged back as far as he could against the end wall, crouching low. Then as another stone crashed down, missing him by inches, he straightened up, a cocked gun in each hand. Better to rush into the open and die fighting than to be squashed like a bug under a boot. He tensed to spring over the crumpled body of the dead outlaw.

In the growth overhead sounded a stutter of gunfire, then Sheriff Harding's voice.

"We're coming, Slade! After 'em boys, don't let 'em get away!"

The brush quivered to a drumroll of shots. Slade leaped to the mouth of the crevice and even as he cleared the walls, the shooting posse tore into view, young Ed Grumley in the forefront. He gave a joyous whoop as he sighted Slade, threw up his gun and let drive at a figure dodging in and out through the brush. The fleeing outlaw went end over end and brought up in a sprawling heap against a tree trunk. Grumley halted, grinning at Slade, as Sheriff Harding came charging around a bush, stuffing cartridges into his gun.

"Guess I got the last one," Grumley told him. "Don't see any more. And Slade's okay."

"Better make sure," said Harding. "Beat the bush and see if there's any more snakes to be smoked out."

The deputies spread out through the chaparral but soon came straggling back.

"Looks like a clean sweep," one reported. "We counted nine carcasses, including a couple Slade must have did for before we got here. And there are nine horses tied back in the brush."

"Fine!" applauded the sheriff. "Slade, you're a good-luck piece. This is the best haul we've ever made. Another one or two like this and we'll clean up the Murrieta outfit."

"And if it hadn't been for Slade catching on like he did, we'd have bulged right smack into that ambush and got blown from under our hats," Grumley declared.

"Well," Slade smiled, "you sort of evened up the score. You got here at just the right time. Things were getting a mite warm."

"We figured they would be when we heard the shooting

start," Harding said with a chuckle. "So we skalleyhooted up the sag as fast as we could."

The bodies were dragged from the brush and laid out in a row. Slade contemplated them thoughtfully.

"Nine," he remarked, "and Wilkins only spoke of eight at the outside."

"Say!" Grumley exclaimed. "I've seen this one before, this one with the crumpled ear that looks like a breed."

"Where?" asked the sheriff.

"He was working in the Alhambra, Amado Fuentes' place. He was swamping there," Grumley replied.

Sheriff Harding looked grim. "I'm not surprised to hear it," he said.

"Did you see him there tonight?" Slade asked Grumley. The deputy shook his head.

"Don't think so," he answered. "Don't recall seeing him of late, but I know I saw him, and only a few days back. I remember because of that ear."

Slade nodded. Struck by a sudden thought, he walked to where the outlaws' horses stood. They were all good animals and in prime condition. He examined their coats carefully.

"This bay was ridden by the hellion who brought the warning to the others," he announced. "Its hide is still slightly sweat-streaked and wet under the saddle flaps, while the others are dry."

He returned to the bodies, squatted beside that of the breed with the crumpled ear and passed his hand over the rough and worn corduroy of the man's britches.

"Come here," he told the sheriff. "Feel inside the thighs. Corduroy absorbs dampness but dissipates it slowly. You'll note the cloth is quite damp. The kind of dampness that comes from a sweating horse. This is the jigger who brought the warning."

"Darned if you aren't right!" exclaimed the sheriff. He glared at the dead breed and tugged his mustache.

"Worked for Fuentes, eh!" he rumbled. "I've been looking sideways at that horned toad for quite a while. Now I'm beginning to believe folks may be right in what they're saying."

"That this fellow worked for Fuentes is no proof that Fuentes is tied up with the outfit," Slade said. "He may have just been hanging around in the Alhambra when Wilkins barged in with his story."

"Reckon you're right," Harding conceded reluctantly. "Anyhow we did a good chore this morning. Nine! And I understand you did for three over in the Mohave—oh, it's the same bunch, all right—and your horse stomped one to death. Makes an even dozen, plus one. Not even Murrieta can take much more of that."

Slade was studying the distorted faces of the dead outlaws.

"Typical Border scum, mean and hard and salty, with little intelligence. I'm afraid whoever runs the outfit is not here."

"Wouldn't argue the point," said Harding, "but at this rate he won't have any outfit to run before long."

"That sort of a head grows a new body mighty fast," Slade retorted.

"You're right," the sheriff admitted gloomily. "Well, I guess we might as well be getting back to town. Rope the carcasses on the horses and let's go."

The City of the Angels seethed with excitement when the grim cavalcade threaded its way through the crowded streets. The bodies were laid out for inspection in the sheriff's office. Soon a stream of the curious was filing in and out.

However, nobody was able to recognize any of the slain bandits, or were discreetly vague. Slade gathered that nobody was particularly anxious to possibly incur the enmity of the dreaded Joaquin Murrieta and his men.

Old Tad Wilkins, the partner of the murdered prospectors, looked the bodies over carefully, his brows drawing together querulously.

"Well, what do you say, Tad?" asked the sheriff. "These the devils?"

"Yep, it's them," Wilkins replied, "only I'm scairt you're short one."

"Short one?"

"Uh-huh. All these fellers are sort of short fellers. I don't think one of 'em is up to six feet."

"What the devil's that got to do with it?" snorted the sheriff.

"Just this," answered Wilkins, "the feller who 'peared to be directin' things and giving orders to the others was a big tall feller; he was over six feet, I'll bet."

"The devil he was!" exclaimed the sheriff. "Did you get a good look at him?'

"Not too good," said Wilkins. "You see, I couldn't get overly close."

Walt Slade spoke for the first time. "Do you think you would recognize him if you saw him again?"

Wilkins hesitated, a queer expression fleeting across his wrinkled countenance. A strained, slightly perplexed expression, Slade thought.

"Maybe I would, especially if he happened to be dressed like he was there at the camp," the prospector finally replied. There was sweat on his face and his eyes were uncertain.

Slade concluded that the old fellow knew more than he cared to mention. In fact he believed that Wilkins had a very good notion who the bandit leader was but that he was appalled, even incredulous in his own mind at what he had learned, and therefore reluctant to speak out.

And Slade decided not to press him, to await a more propitious time for further questioning.

In this decision El Halcon made a mistake.

FOURTEEN

IT WAS NEARLY DARK before Slade and Sheriff Harding found time to get something to eat. Together they walked to the Square Deal, found a vacant table and gave their order to a waiter.

Grumley and the other deputies had spread the story of the happenings in the canyon and Slade found himself the recipient of salutations and admiring glances from all sides. Dave Lang, the tall handsome owner of the Square Deal, came over and dropped into a vacant chair.

"I want to compliment you, Mr. Slade," he said in his deep and resonant voice. "The way you outsmarted those devils was wonderful. Smart and fast thinking. I've a notion that Murrieta, if it really was part of his outfit, is saying things about you right now that wouldn't make nice hearing.

"But don't underestimate Murrieta," he added. "The original Joaquin Murrieta was bad enough, with his mocking 'Buenos noches, Señor!' just before he killed his victim, but he was not remarkable for brains. And brains are something I don't think our Joaquin Murrieta lacks. He'll sure be on the prod against all of you, and you in particular, Mr. Slade."

"You believe there really is a Joaquin Murrieta?" Slade asked curiously.

"No doubt in my mind," said Lang. "Or rather, there is a very smart, salty and utterly ruthless outlaw leader operating in this section. He, whoever he is, never called himself Murrieta, so far as I have ever heard; the name was hung on him by others. But he has intelligence and imagination not usually associated with his kind."

Slade did not argue with the statement. The patience and ingenuity displayed in the planning and setting of the ambush was proof of what Lang maintained. And he was prepared to take the saloonkeeper's friendly warning in good faith; it would be foolish to underestimate Murrieta.

Sheriff Harding sipped the drink a waiter had brought him. "Maybe the larruping we gave him will slow him down for a spell," he observed. "Altogether, since Slade hit California we've accounted for thirteen of his sidewinders. Fourteen, if you count Slow Baker who, I figure, was tied up with Murrieta."

Lang shook his head, his brilliant eyes roving over the busy room. "Murrieta will find plenty more to draw from," he predicted. "In my opinion, he's got a firm grip on all the lawless elements of this section, and that means plenty. And I've a notion," he added with a quick smile, "that folks will be mighty surprised when and if they learn who Murrieta really is.'

"I've a notion I won't be," growled the sheriff. Lang smiled again and beckoned the waiter who was hovering about.

"The check," he said. The waiter handed it to him. Lang placed it on the table and bent his golden head over it. Taking a pencil from his pocket, he wrote something.

Walt Slade was sitting directly opposite Lang. Abruptly the concentration furrow deepened between his black brows.

Lang straightened up and handed the check to the waiter. "Everything is on the house, gentlemen," he said as he rose to his feet. "Eat and drink hearty; we don't often get a chance for a celebration like this." With a smile and a nod he turned and sauntered across the crowded room, pausing at tables from time to time or at one of the games. Slade's thoughtful gaze followed his progress until he reached the far end of the bar.

Slade and the sheriff enjoyed Dave Lang's hospitality to the extent of a good dinner and a couple of drinks. After which Harding shoved back his glass and stood up.

"I'm going up to bed," he announced. "Without a wink of sleep last night, I feel tuckered. Guess they'll want to hold another inquest tomorrow. Be at the office about noon."

"I'll be there," Slade promised.

After the sheriff departed, Slade rolled a cigarette, sat

back in his chair and searched the crowded room with his eyes. He hoped to spot old Tad Wilkins and have a little talk with him. But the prospector was nowhere to be seen. Slade debated whether to look for him in some of the other saloons but decided against it. No telling where the old fellow had gotten to, and tomorow would do just as well. He waved goodnight to Dave Lang at the end of the bar and headed for bed.

It seemed to Slade that he had been asleep for a few minutes when he was aroused by a hammering on the door.

"It's me, Ed Grumley," a voice called. "Let me in."

Slade opened the door and Grumley entered. "Sheriff wants you over to his office, right away," he said.

"Something happen?" Slade asked as he began throwing on his clothes.

"Must have, but I don't know what," Grumley replied. "He roused me up and told me to come get you—I sleep right across from the office."

Slade buckled on his double cartridge belts. "Let's go," he said.

They found Sheriff Harding seated at his desk. The lines in his face seemed deeper and Slade thought he suddenly looked very tired and old.

"Much obliged, Grumley," he said. "You can go back to bed now. Be here tomorrow around twelve."

Grumley cast a startled glance at the couch on the far side of the room, but he only nodded and said, "Okay." He closed the door very softly.

The bodies of the outlaws had been removed, but another body lay on the couch. Sheriff Harding gestured to it.

"Tad Wilkins," he said.

Slade stared. "What happened to him?"

"They picked him up in the mouth of the alley that runs in back of that blasted Alhambra," replied the sheriff. "Folks heard shooting and went to see what it was about, and there he was, with two bullets through his back. He wasn't quite dead so they high-tailed to get me and Doc Cooper. Doc and I got there about the same time, but Tad passed on before Doc could do anything for him."

Slade walked to the couch and gazed down at the prospector's dead face.

"Poor old fellow!" he said, adding bitterly, "And I blame myself for this."

"Why?" asked the sheriff in astonishment.

"Wilkins knew something, and I sensed he knew it," Slade explained. "I planned to question him, but put it off, and as a result somebody closed his mouth with a slug. I should have had a talk with him when he was here at the office in the afternoon. Then we could have made provisions for his safety, if what I believed was true."

"What did he know?" asked the sheriff.

"I think," Slade said slowly, "that the devil known as Murrieta made one of the stupid mistakes the outlaw fraternity always makes, sooner or later. He planned to have Wilkins learn of the robbing and murdering of his partners, reasoning, and rightly, that Wilkins would immediately come to you and that you would fall into the cleverly laid trap Murrieta had devised for you. But Murrieta allowed Wilkins to get a mite too close to the camp. Wilkins either recognized him or noted a remarkable resemblance to somebody he knew well. Here in the office this afternoon he seemed stunned, hardly able to believe, in his own mind, what he had learned. Yes, I think he recognized Murrieta and was utterly astounded. So much so that he hesitated to talk about it. I think, however, that I'd have been able to get the truth from him if I'd moved quickly enough. Now it's too late."

"You could be right," admitted the sheriff. "And I'm going to tell you something that makes me believe you are right. Tad said a few words to me before he went unconscious and died."

"What did he say?" Slade asked.

"He said, and I'll repeat it just as he said it, 'Fuentes—find Fuentes—he—', then his voice trailed off in a mumble. He never finished whatever it was he tried to say. What do you think?"

"I think," Slade said, "that we should have a talk with Fuentes."

"That's the way I felt about it, but I wanted your opinion," said the sheriff. "And I wanted you to go with me. You're still a deputy, you know."

Slade nodded, contemplating the old peace officer. He had come to a certain decision. He was positive that Branch Harding was trustworthy and close-mouthed. He slipped the badge of the Rangers from its pocket in his broad leather belt and laid it on the desk.

Sheriff Harding regarded the famous silver star set on a silver circle, the symbol of law and order and justice, and did not appear remarkably surprised.

"I been thinking as much," he said. "Wyatt Earp didn't say you were a Texas Ranger, because he didn't know for sure, I reckon. But it wasn't hard to figure what he thought. Well, that star gives you an official standing, even though it doesn't pack any official authority under California law. But your deputy sheriff's badge does, in Los Angeles County. Let's go see Fuentes."

When they arrived at the Alhambra, Amado Fuentes wasn't in sight.

"He left a little while ago," the head bartender answered the sheriff's question as to the owner's whereabouts. "Said he was going upstairs to his rooms. Reckon you'll find him there."

A door near the corner of the building opened onto steps that led to the second floor. Slade and Harding mounted the stairs to a lighted hallway where the sheriff knocked on a door.

There was no answer. He knocked again, harder. Silence still persisted beyond the closed door. Harding seized the knob and turned it. The door swung open, revealing a room dimly lighted by a small lamp. There was nobody in the room, nor in the two that adjoined it. Everything appeared to be in order, with no signs of a hurried departure.

"Now where did that hellion get to?" the sheriff wondered in exasperated tones.

Slade thought a moment. "Do you know where Fuentes keeps his horse?"

"Uh-huh, right around the corner a piece," replied Harding.

"Let's go and see if he's been there," Slade suggested.

"A good notion," grunted the sheriff and led the way to the stable.

Repeated pounding on the door finally brought a white-haired crusty old fellow who regarded them with scant favor.

"What's the big notion, waking people up at this time of night?" he demanded. "This makes two times tonight and I'm getting tired of it."

Sheriff Harding ignored the question. "See anything of Amado Fuentes tonight, has he been here?"

"Nope," replied the stablekeeper. "His horse ain't here either. A feller came and got it just a little while ago. Brought a note from Fuentes telling me to give it to him; he's done that before. Feller said he worked for Fuentes. Something wrong?"

"I don't know yet," replied Harding. "Feller brought a note, you said?"

"Uh-huh. I didn't think anything of it. Fuentes is always sending for his horse at ungodly hours. He used to be a cowhand before he got in the likker business, you know. Does a heap of riding around."

The sheriff glanced at Slade.

"Let's go," the Ranger said. "By the way, what did the man who brought the note look like?" he asked the keeper.

"Sort of ganglin' and rather tall," the oldster replied. "Thin face. I didn't pay much attention to him."

Slade nodded. "Let's go," he repeated to the sheriff.

After they had left the stable, Slade asked, "Did anybody else hear Wilkins' last words?"

"Reckon the folks crowding around did," admitted Harding. "There were several of 'em leaning over me. But I doubt if they heard it all—I barely heard the last part with my ear right against his mouth. The last part was just a mumble."

"But they could have heard the first word he spoke— 'Fuentes'?"

"Yep, they could have heard that," agreed the sheriff.

"And Fuentes sent for his horse," Slade remarked.

"What does it mean?" asked the sheriff.

"It could mean a good deal, and it may mean nothing," Slade replied. "The keeper said Fuentes was in the habit of riding off at odd times, perhaps to get away from his business and relax, as a man who has always done a great deal of riding can. If so, he should be back sooner or later, probably sooner."

"And if he doesn't come back?"

"Then," Slade said grimly, "it will be up to us to learn why. Let's go to bed."

FIFTEEN

SLADE SLEPT LATE and when he arrived at the Square Deal for breakfast, he found the place seething with excitement. Garbled versions of Tad Wilkins' last utterances were flying about and men were openly declaring that Amado Fuentes was responsible for the killing. The answer to those who sought to defend the Alhambra owner was,

"If he didn't have anything to do with it, why did he cut and run like he did?"

From which Slade gathered that Fuentes had not yet put in an appearance. He listened to people insisting that Wilkins had named Fuentes his killer with his dying breath. There was a lot of wild talk going on and Slade decided that if Fuentes did suddenly reappear, he might well need some official protection. Tad Wilkins, always a successful prospector, had been a free spender and was well known and popular. Those who had been his friends and associates were in an ugly mood. He was thoughtful when he made his way to the sheriff's office and the inquest.

The coroner's jury dealt briefly with the slain outlaws, holding that the killings were justified and a good chore. The Wilkins case, however, was lengthy, provoking much discussion, some of it acrimonious. After prolonged debate the jury rendered a verdict which said Wilkins had met his death at the hands of a person or persons unknown, but that Sheriff Harding would do well to locate Amado Fuentes and find out what he knew about the matter.

The head bartender at the Alhambra vigorously defended the absent owner, as did other employees.

"Something bad has happened to Amado," the bartender declared. "I'll bet my last peso on that. Sheriff, I

97

know you haven't much use for him and hold that his place is a hangout for questionable characters, but can you see Amado Fuentes shooting an old man in the back?"

"I certainly wouldn't have believed it of him," Harding was forced to admit. "But," he added, "under certain circumstances a man will do things you'd never expect him to. Remember, Pete, I'm not accusing Fuentes of anything; it is not my place to do so. I'm a law enforcement officer, not a prosecutor. Poor old Tad's last words put Fuentes sort of under a cloud, and it would be the sensible thing for him to come forward and try and explain why Tad called his name that way. Why don't he come forward?"

"I'd say because he can't," the bartender retorted grimly. "I hate to say it, but I'm mighty, mighty scairt that when you find Amado you won't find him alive."

"And what do you think of that?" the sheriff asked Slade, as the bartender moved away for a moment.

"It's something to think on," Slade replied.

Slade was thinking on something else, something that intrigued him. Nobody appeared able, from the old stable-keeper's meagre description, to identify the man who had brought the note requesting Fuentes' horse.

"We've had lots of jiggers working here," said the bartender, "but I can't seem to place anybody who looked like that. One thing's sure for certain, he ain't working here now."

Which Slade thought was significant. Of course, the possibility that Fuentes, wanting to keep out of sight, had sent somebody for the horse who could be trusted to keep his mouth shut afterward was not to be discounted. That, however, presupposed that Fuentes had a good reason for staying under cover and getting out of town as quickly as possible.

"Maybe he took a long ride and spent the night out," the sheriff suggested when they discussed the matter. "If so, he'll be showing up any time now. We'll wait and see."

They waited. The day passed, and the evening, with no sign of the Alhambra owner.

"Beginning to look bad for Fuentes," commented Harding.

"Yes, it does, in one way or another," Slade acceded.

Around midnight the sheriff announced his intention of going to bed.

"Doesn't seem possible any more to get a good night's rest," he growled. "Maybe I can get one tonight. I sure need it."

Slade nodded agreement. The old man did look terribly weary.

"I expect I'll follow your example before long," he said. "See you tomorrow."

Slade did retire to his room shortly afterward. Not feeling particularly sleepy, however, without lighting the lamp he drew a chair to a window and sat down to smoke. The alley below was quite dark save where a glow from the open door of the little restaurant diagonally across the street cast a bar of radiance. As Slade was finishing his second cigarette, he saw a man leave the restaurant and head up the alley. He watched idly as the shadowy form drew near, halted, then crossed to the stable door. A knock sounded and Juan Vergara, who was still pottering about the stalls, opened the door. A low-voiced conversation that Slade could not catch ensued. The stranger entered and Vergara closed the door. A moment later there was a knock at the door of his room.

"That you, Juan?" he called.

"Yes," answered Vergara's voice. "There's a fellow downstairs wants to see you."

Slade opened the door and accompanied Vergara down stairs. The visitor was a stocky, bearded individual dressed in the blue shirt, worn corduroys and laced boots favored by the miners and prospectors.

"Howdy?" he greeted. "You the deputy sheriff?"

"One of them," Slade replied.

"Feller who runs the restaurant down the street told me there was a deputy staying here," the man said. "I tried to find the sheriff but couldn't—somebody said they reckoned he'd gone to bed. I got into town a couple of hours back and heard tell of Tad Wilkins getting killed. I knew old Tad well. Then I heard you law fellers wanted to see Amado Fuentes who's been missing all day. I saw Fuentes last night, along toward morning."

"Yes? Where?" Slade asked.

"Up in Klamath Canyon," the man replied.

"Klamath Canyon?" Slade repeated. "Where's that?"

"First canyon you come to after passing White Horse Canyon on the north trail," the other answered. "About five miles north of White Horse. Trail runs right past its mouth."

"And you say you saw Fuentes there?"

"Yep, him and two other fellers riding up the canyon."

"Did you speak to him?"

"Nope," the man said. "I was coming down the canyon —been washing out dust up there for a couple of months, got a purty good poke—when I heard horses coming up the canyon. When you hear folks riding toward you in those gulleys at night and you're alone by yourself, you don't bulge right ahead and meet 'em. Ain't healthy, the way things have been going of late. So I backed my mule and my pack mule into the brush and waited for them to get past. Right when they came by where I was holed up—there was three of 'em—the feller riding in the middle struck a match to a cigarette and I got a look at his face. It was Fuentes, all right. I've seen him lots of times.

"I started to let out a yelp to him, then decided not to. I hadn't got any look at the other two fellers and sometimes gents have easy trigger fingers, especially when somebody bellers at 'em from the dark. So I just let 'em ride past and then moseyed on my way down the canyon. No water up there and I wanted to get out and across the trail to the west where there's a crik. Didn't have but a couple of miles to go to the canyon mouth. I made my camp and rested up all day and headed for town when it began to get cool."

"Where does that canyon lead to?" Slade asked.

"Runs sort of northeast through the hills and opens out not far from the Sacramento Valley Trail, the trail that runs right up to Sacramento City. Mighty rough in there or it would be a good short-cut to the Sacramento," the miner replied.

Slade nodded. "Thank you for bringing me the word," he said. "It may prove very important."

The other ducked his head and turned to the door. "Thought you fellers would want to know about it," he said, and took his departure. "Well," observed Vergara, after the door had closed on their visitor, "looks like maybe Fuentes really is pulling out of the section."

"Possibly," Slade conceded. Vergera shot him a keen look.

"What do you think?" he asked.

"It may be a trap," Slade answered. "But if it is, I'll know it before I ride up that canyon."

"You're going up there, then?"

"Yes," Slade said. "I'm curious."

"You'll be taking an awful chance, riding up there alone," protested Vergara. "If I didn't have to take care of the horses I'd go with you."

"Thanks, but I'll make out okay," Slade answered. "There's one thing you can do for me, though, if you will. In the morning find Sheriff Harding and repeat what the fellow told us, and tell him I'm up there."

"I will," Vegara promised.

As he got the rig on Shadow, Slade debated whether he should himself notify the sheriff before heading for the canyon, then decided against it. The old man was worn out and needed his rest. Let him sleep. He threaded his way through the nearly deserted side streets and rode north.

"Shadow," he observed, "there's one little thing that struck me as sort of funny. That jigger took it for granted I'd know the exact location of White Horse Canyon and be able to place Klamath in relation to it. Why would he think I'd know the location of White Horse Canyon? Of course he might have been talking with somebody who mentioned what happened in White Horse Canyon day before yesterday, but right now the chief topic of conversation everywhere is Tad Wilkins and Amado Fuentes. May mean nothing, but just the same it's got me thinking."

Slade rode steadily; he passed the dark mouth of White Horse Canyon and continued north. Just as dawn was breaking he reached another cleft in the hills which he reasoned must be Klamath. Keeping close to the brush-grown slope on his right, he continued until he came to where a narrow, chaparral-crowded track ran from the gorge to join the broader trail he was riding. Here he pulled up, hooked one long leg over the saddle horn and rolled a cigarette, waiting for the light to strengthen a bit. After a while he pinched out the butt and dismounted.

Back and forth he quartered the ground, studying its surface intently. There had been heavy rain recently and in the sheltered gorge the ground was still quite soft. He found prints of horses' hoofs, not more than twenty-four hours old, he estimated. He decided that four horses had recently passed up the canyon together, not three as the informant had stated. But nowhere did he find the narrower prints of mule shoes coming down the canyon. Slade straightened up and returned to his horse.

"They slipped, feller," he told the black. "Yes, they made one of the little slips the owlhoot brand always makes. They didn't figure on me looking for mule tracks to corroborate that bewhiskered liar's yarn. He said he came down the canyon on muleback. He lied. Chances are he wasn't up in this direction at all but passed on to me the yarn which was handed him by whoever concocted it. Seems somebody is mighty anxious for me to ride up this crack in the hills. Well, I wouldn't think of disappointing them. Let's go, feller, but keep your eyes open and your ears pricked."

Shadow snorted. Slade chuckled and swung into the saddle.

Slade rode slowly up the silent, shadowy gorge, giving careful attention to the line of prints stretching out before him. They continued steadily, evenly spaced.

Birds, of which California boasts a multitude, went about their business in and over the brush without alarm. Now and then a rabbit or some little rodent would hop along the trail or from one side would stare dubiously at the horseman before whisking away. Slade rode on.

The trail had a steady upward slope and as it climbed higher, the gorge widened. Which indicated, Slade thought, that its east mouth was not far off. He slowed Shadow a bit.

Abruply the hoof prints swerved to the right, toward the south wall of the canyon. They entered a narrow opening in the growth, which here was somewhat thinner, especially at the edges of what appeared to be a trail leading to the south wall of the canyon. Slade pulled up.

Somewhere along that game track which wormed through the brush would be the ambush, if there was one. The place was ideal for drygulching.

Motionless in the shadow of the growth, Slade debated just what to do. Somewhere ahead were three or four desperate men, possibly more. If he went barging into their hole-up he could expect nothing but disaster. In any event the odds were heavily against him.

"Well, here goes," he told Shadow. "First thing is to hole you up somewhere, then we'll see."

He noted a thin place in the growth that hemmed the trail and headed Shadow at the spot. The big black pushed his way through tangle, blowing with disgust but proceeding steadily. In a tiny cleared spot where grass grew Slade drew rein and dismounted. He flipped the bit loose so that the horse could graze in comfort.

"Okay, feller, stay put," he ordered, "but if I call for you, come a-running."

Perhaps Shadow understood, perhaps he didn't, but there was no doubt in Slade's mind that he'd know exactly what to do did his master call.

Slade returned to the opening in the growth and studied it intently. He noted that the trail apparently curved steadily to the east, which meant that a possible watcher would certainly hole up on the east side of the trail, where he could look along the cord of the bow. With a final glance around, Slade entered the growth nearly a dozen yards to the east of the trail. He wormed his way slowly and silently through the thick brush, pausing often. He had covered perhaps a hundred yards when he halted sharply. To his sensitive nostrils had come the unmistakeable tang of wood smoke.

For several moments he stood motionless, sweeping the growth on his right with his eyes. Nothing moved there and there was no sound to denote occupancy. He resumed his stealthy progress. The smell of smoke grew stronger.

Abruptly he halted again. His keen ears had caught a sound, a restless rustle, as of a man shifting a cramped position and brushing against the encroaching chaparral. The sound came from slightly ahead and to the right. He glided forward a few more steps and paused, peering toward the trail. Then with hardly perceptible movement he edged to the right.

He covered half a dozen yards, and stood motionless. Almost within arm's reach he saw a man crouching behind a screen of brush, his eyes fixed intently on the curve of the trail beyond his shelter. Slade could make out the slim shape of the rifle he held at the ready, waiting for him to show around the bend.

Slade drew his right-hand gun, gripped the stock firmly, and took a long stride forward. The watcher leaped erect and whirled around at the rustle of his step. The rifle jumped to his shoulder.

El Halcon struck with all the strength of his powerful arm and shoulder back of the blow. The gun barrel landed with a sodden, crunching sound. The fellow gave a gasp and sank to the ground, the rifle falling from his loosened grip. His limbs jerked grotesquely, he stiffened, relaxed, and did not move again. Slade leaned forward, the gun poised. But there was no need for a second blow. The steel barrel of the heavy Colt had cracked the fellow's skull like an eggshell.

"One down and three to go!" he muttered. Holstering his gun, he resumed his cautious progress toward the strengthening smell of smoke.

Another hundred paces and the growth began to thin. Slade peered through a final fringe at a fairly wide clearing. From the south a second and wider trail opened into it, and a little more than fifty feet from where he stood was a small weatherbeaten cabin, doubtless an abandoned miner's shack, the like of which dotted the California hills and valleys. From its stick-and-mud chimney rose a trickle of smoke.

Slade studied the building. To the west and to the south the growth which hemmed the clearing was a good two hundred yards distant, but on the east it grew down almost to the rear wall of the shack. A window faced to the north but the panes were so streaked with dirt that he could not see into the cabin.

However, very likely those inside could see out well enough to spot anybody crossing the open space from the growth to the building. Such an approach would be altogether too risky even to consider. He continued to survey the cabin and its surroundings, his attention concentrated on the thick growth crowding the rear wall.

"If the darn shack just has a back door!" he muttered.

Silently, he circled around through the chaparral until he was opposite the rear of the building, then he stole forward. With a throb of exultation he saw the cabin did have a back door, and that it stood slightly ajar. He continued his advance, hands hovering over the butts of his guns, until he reached the door. He halted, listening.

Voices were sounding inside the building. One, rather high-pitched and musical but raspingly hoarse, as if the speaker had a dry throat, was vaguely familiar.

"For God's sake! Why don't you kill me and get it over with!" the voice was saying. "I wouldn't have believed that even Murrieta would go in for this sort of torture."

"You'll get killed soon enough, so don't let it worry you," said another and harsher voice. "We're just waiting for Holt to bring in the other hellion. Then soon as the boss gets here, which won't be long, we'll take care of both of you."

"Like a nice cold drink?" jeered another voice which was answered by what sounded like a moan.

Slade un-leathered both guns, drew back, lunged forward and hit the door with his shoulder. It flew open with a crash and he was in the single room of the cabin.

Seated in a heavy home-made chair, to the legs of which his ankles were securely lashed, his hands bound behind him, his face gray and haggard, was Amado Fuentes. At a table holding a bottle and tin cups were two men who leaped to their feet to stare open-mouthed at the tall Ranger. The bottle fell over on its side and whisky gushed out onto the floor.

"Elevate! You're covered!" Slade thundered at them. He took a sideways step to get out of line with Fuentes and his foot came down in the puddle of spilled whiskey. He slipped, reeled off balance.

The outlaws went for their irons. The cabin rocked to a roar of gunfire.

One man went down, screaming hoarsely, blood gushing from his bullet-slashed throat. The other lined sights with Slade's breast but before he could pull the trigger, Fuentes hurled himself forward, chair and all, to strike the fellow just above the knees. His gun exploded, the bullet went wild. Slade fired two shots, left and right.

The outlaw plunged forward on his face to lie gasping and retching, his life draining out through his shattered lungs. Blood oozing from a bullet-burned cheek and drip-

ping from the fingers of his left hand, Slade holstered his
guns, whipped a knife from his pocket and sprang to
where Fuentes was bumping and floundering on the
floor. A few slashes freed him. He tried to rise but fell
back, writhing with the agony of returning circulation
in his numbed limbs. Slade picked him up and laid him
on a bunk against one wall.

"Water!" he croaked. "For God's sake, water! In the
bucket! Water!"

Slade plucked the bucket from the floor, filled a tin
cup and held it to Fuentes' cracked and blackened lips.
He drank in great gulps. Slade refilled the cup and
Fuentes drained it. He struggled to get hold of the
bucket, but Slade drew it away from him.

"Take it easy," he cautioned. "You'll be sick. Wait,
I see something better."

A rusty iron stove stood in one corner of the room.
On it was a coffeepot with a wisp of steam rising from
its spout. Slade filled the cup and held it for Fuentes to
swallow.

"Lie back and relax a minute," Slade told him. "I want
a look at that hellion on the floor. I think he's still alive."
He stooped and turned the dying man over on his back.
The outlaw glared up at him with hate-filled eyes.

"You're taking the Big Jump, fellow," Slade said. "Why
not come clean before you go and make it easier for
yourself? Who is the head of your outfit?"

"G—go to hell!" the outlaw gasped, and died.

SIXTEEN

SLADE WENT BACK to Fuentes, who was sitting up, massaging his bruised and swollen wrists. He stared at Slade.

"You're hurt!" he exclaimed. "You're bleeding."

"Scratches," Slade replied. "Bullet nicked my arm. What happened to you, and how'd you get here?"

"I hardly know," Fuentes answered. "I'd gone to my rooms to get something, a short while after hearing about Tad Wilkins being shot. When I stepped out the door somebody belted me over the head with a pistol barrel or something; knocked me cold. Next thing I knew I was roped to the saddle of my own horse with a hellion leading it by the bridle and a couple more riding beside me. When I started to talk they threatened to beat my brains out if I didn't shut up. They brought me here and tied me in that infernal chair. That was yesterday morning. They kept me tied and wouldn't give me food or water. I thought I was going mad. They took turns at watching the trail this morning, while the other two stayed with me. They seemed positive you would show up on the trail and figured to grab you. They were going to kill us both as soon as some devil they called the 'boss' got here."

"Didn't mention his name?"

"No, they just called him the 'boss'." Fuentes suddenly glanced around apprehensively. "He's liable to get here any minute, from what they said."

Slade nodded. "We've got to move, pronto," he said. "Think you can ride?"

"I'll make out," Fuentes said, rising to his feet and walking rather shakily across the room to the coffee pot. "One more swig and I'll be ready to go. I think my horse is under a lean-to at the side of the shack. That's where they left him."

"Okay," Slade said. "Let's get out of here."

"The bay's mine," said Fuentes when they reached the lean-to, under which four horses stood. "And that's my saddle in the corner."

Slade got the rig on the bay with speed. "Up with you," he directed, "I'll get my critter."

He ran swiftly to where the trail he had ridden entered the clearing and whistled. A few minutes later hoofs pattered and Shadow cantered in, blowing and snorting.

"That's a *horse!*" exclaimed Fuentes.

"He'll do," Slade said as he flipped the bit in place and mounted. "He— Ride, fellow, ride! Trail, Shadow!"

From the south trail which cut the far side of the clearing, half a dozen riders bulged into view. In the forefront was a tall broad-shouldered man whose face was but a whitish blur against the background of dark growth.

A volley of startled yells sounded, then a deep and powerful voice rose above the din.

"*Let them have it!*"

With Shadow going at full speed, Slade hunched low as bullets sang past. Fuentes yelped as one grained his shoulder. Another twitched at Slade's sleeve like an urgent hand. Then they were tearing between the walls of growth and out of range around the curve of the trail.

"Ride!" Slade shouted to his companion. "Get everything you can out of that nag! They're after us!"

Fuentes obeyed, flogging his horse with his hand. Shadow easily kept pace, Slade talking to him soothingly. Behind sounded a thudding of hoofs and yells and curses. A few minutes later they swerved around a final bend and fled west through Klamath Canyon, the outlaws thundering in pursuit.

Coming up the canyon, Slade had been exasperated by the trail's many twists and turns; now he blessed them. The pursuers were close, darned close, but the bends were so many and abrupt that so far they were unable to sight the fugitives.

But Slade knew this state of affairs could not last. Fuentes' horse was a good one but not remarkable for speed. Shadow could have easily outdistanced the outlaws but Slade had to hold him back in deference to his companion's slower pace. And his ears told him the pursuit was slowly closing the distance. Directly ahead the trail straightened out for more than a hundred yards before it curved again.

"Ride!" Slade shouted. "We've got to reach the bend before they show. Ride!"

Fuentes belabored his horse, the bend drew near. Just before they reached it, Slade pulled Shadow to a slithering halt. He was out of the saddle, his Winchester gripped in his hands, while Shadow was still in motion. Fuentes, yelling protest, went careening around the curve, his maddened horse refusing to obey his pull on the reins. Slade dropped to one knee and waited, the rifle butt clamped against his shoulder.

Around the bend flashed the pursuers. The rifle muzzle gushed flame. A man spun from the saddle. Another shot, and a second outlaw fell. Slade, bullets clipping the leaves over his head, fired a third time. The tall leader, whose face he still could not see plainly, slewed sideways, gripping the horn for support. He straightened, jerked his horse to a halt and spun it around. His companions likewise turned their mounts. Slade fired two more shots and heard a yell of pain before they vanished around the bend. He mounted Shadow and sent him down canyon to meet Fuentes coming back.

"Come on," Slade told him. "I think that will hold them for a while—got two and winged a couple more, including the head devil of the lot or I'm a heap mistaken. Ride! I won't feel right till we're a long way down the North Trail."

They rode as fast as the bay could go. An hour later they reached the broad North Trail and turned south. Slade heaved a sigh of relief. The trail was pretty well travelled in the daytime and he did not believe the outlaws would continue the chase along it, even though they might pick reserves somewhere. He slowed Shadow and turned to his companion.

"Fuentes," he said, "have you any notion why you were kidnapped?"

"Slade, I haven't the slightest idea," Fuentes replied. "I've made some enemies, of course; a man in my business always does. But I can't conceive of any of them going in for a thing like that."

"Would anybody profit by your being put out of the picture?"

"Nobody I can think of, except my old father up in Sacramento City, who would inherit the business. But I can't see him going in for murder to get it."

"I imagine we can eliminate him as a suspect," Slade smiled.

"To me the whole affair just doesn't make sense," Fuentes said.

"Perhaps not," Slade answered. "But then again, perhaps it does."

Fuentes stared at him questioningly but Slade did not see fit to amplify his cryptic remark.

In fact, El Halcon was getting a notion. A notion that on the face of it appeared so absurd that he didn't care to mention it to his companion or anybody else yet. He rode on in silence.

They had covered but a few miles when they saw a body of men riding swiftly toward them. Slade recognized Sheriff Harding, Ed Grumley and other deputies and specials. Very quickly they met.

"So you got him, eh?" said the sheriff, reining in his blowing horse.

"Yes, I got him," Slade replied.

"And a mighty good thing for me he did," Fuentes said.

Sheriff Harding appeared somewhat nonplussed at the attitude of the pair, which was certainly not that of captor and captive. The deputies also looked bewildered.

"Slade," Harding said, "won't you tell us what it's all about?"

Slade told him. The sheriff swore. "I'm going loco," he declared. "And no wonder. If that isn't the dad-blamest thing. Figured to do away with Fuentes and leave everybody thinking he killed Tad Wilkins."

"Would have served a double purpose," Slade pointed out. "Would have gotten Fuentes out of the way of whoever wants him out of the way, and shifted possible suspicion from whoever it was killed Wilkins. Well, let's head for town. Fuentes is starved and I feel a mite lank myself. You can send somebody to pick up the bodies tomorrow, Sheriff, if you are of a mind to."

"Reckon I'll have to," growled the sheriff. "Somebody

might spot one of the skunks. Anyhow, the Murrieta bunch has taken a thinning out, one way or another, since you hit the section. About eighteen, so far, the way I number it. I don't see how there can be many more of the devils left. Let's go!"

When they reached the City of the Angels, Slade looked after his horse, attended to the slight wound in his arm and then repaired to the Alhambra to join Fuentes and the others.

"Everything on the house," said the owner. "I figure it'll take two cooks to fill me up. I'm empty as a gutted sparrow."

Fuentes, naturally strong and vigorous, was recuperating nicely from his experience. His wrists and ankles were still swollen and painful, but otherwise he appeared little the worse for wear.

The story of what had happened quickly got around and Slade smiled to himself as men came to the table to congratulate Fuentes and loudly declare that they never believed for a minute that he was mixed up in anything off-color. Slade himself came in for plenty of comment and discussion at the crowded bar. A gray old waddie summed up the concensus of opinion:

"There are folks who 'low that big feller is a outlaw from Texas himself. Well, if it's so, all I've got to say is that I hope Texas gets busy and sends us a whole regiment of the same sort of outlaws; we can use 'em."

After a bountiful meal, Slade left the Alhambra and moved on to the Square Deal. He found a place at the bar, ordered a drink and glanced around.

"Don't see Lang anywhere," he remarked casually to the bartender who served him.

"He ain't here," the drink juggler replied. "Rode up to his ranch, the Bradded L, to the northwest of town. He spends a good deal of his time there. Wouldn't be surprised if he ends up out of the likker business and goes back to cow raising. Understand he was in that business in Arizona before he settled here. Yep, he's liable to do that, especially if Amado Fuentes happens to beat him out in the election for Mayor. Fuentes could do it; he's got a following and what just happened won't hurt his chances any. Folks kind of cotton to a feller who's come close to getting a raw deal. Last night everybody in here was cussin' Fuentes; this evening they can't say enough good things about him. Well, that's the way the world wags; you're down at the bottom today and up top tomorrow, or the other way around."

The barkeep ambled off to wait on an impatient customer. Slade sipped his drink and studied the crowd. He hung around for some time, but Dave Lang did not put in an appearance. Pretty well worn out by a sleepless night and a turbulent day, he went to bed early and slept until well past sun-up.

After dressing, Slade sat for some time by the window, smoking and thinking. His thoughts dwelt chiefly on the tall man who had called "*Let them have it!*" as he and Fuentes dashed for cover. Of course it could be coincidence, but his voice was remarkably similar to that of the killer who had shouted the identical words in the canyon east of El Paso a moment before the second devastating volley mowed down the unfortunate cowboys who were mining gold in the valley. So much so, in fact, that with the similarity of operation of the outfits taken into account, Slade was pretty well convinced that the Texas robbers and the Murrieta band, or a portion of it, were one and the same. But who the devil was the man in question! Slade had a notion who he was, but was forced to admit he had practically no evidence to bolster a belief that appeared fantastic. Well, future events might provide him the proof he needed. Anyhow, who else, so far as he had been able to learn, would possibly profit from the extinction of Amado Fuentes?

Feeling hungry, he descended the stairs and found Juan Vergara already at work.

"So," said the stablekeeper, "it looks like you figured things right."

"Yes, it was a trap, all right," Slade acceded. "Much obliged for notifying the sheriff. He was a mite late getting there, but if things had worked out a bit differently, I could have used him."

"I looked him up as soon as it got light," Vergara said. "Roused him out of bed. Then I prowled all over town trying to spot that sidewinder who brought you the word, but couldn't find hair or hide of him. I'd sure like to line my sawed-off with the skunk."

After eating his breakfast, Slade found Sheriff Hard-

ing busy at his desk. Taking a chair, he waited for
Harding to finish the paper work that occupied him.
Finally the peace officer folded the documents and shoved
them in a drawer. He raised his eyes to Slade.

"Sent half a dozen deputies to bring in those carcasses,"
he announced. "They should be back before dark. Wonder
if anybody will recognize some of the varmints?"

"Hard to tell, but possible," Slade replied. "Perhaps
somebody will recognize them and be willing to talk. I
don't think the name of Murrieta is such a bogie as it used
to be. I'd say folks are beginning to realize that he and
his bunch are not invulnerable, although the murder of
Wilkins must have been something of a jolt to those who
are really afraid of Murrieta."

"And you believe Tad was killed because he knew
something?"

"No doubt in my mind as to that," Slade insisted. "Perhaps he talked to somebody after he'd had a few drinks
and the talk was overheard by, or was relayed to, the wrong
pair of ears. I'd say, too, that after thinking it over, Wilkins realized that Amado Fuentes was in deadly danger. In
my opinion he was trying to contact Fuentes and warn
him when he was killed. That, of course, is just theory on
my part, but I believe I'm right."

"I've a notion you are," grunted the sheriff.

During the course of the day, Slade visited the Square
Deal a couple of times but Dave Lang still had not put in
an appearance.

Dusk was falling when the deputies rode in with five
bodies roped to the backs of mules. The burdens were
deposited in the sheriff's office. Slade and Harding looked
them over carefully.

"Where did you find this one?" Slade asked Ed Grumley, indicating a bearded individual dressed like a miner
and with a hole between his glazed eyes.

"Picked him up a couple of miles this side of that side
trail to the clearing, him and the lanky one with the
busted nose. Reckon they're the two you lined sights with
when they were chasing you and Fuentes. Why?"

"Because," Slade said, "he's the hellion who brought
me word that he'd spotted Fuentes riding up the canyon."

"By gosh! Looks like there's some justice, after all!"
exclaimed the sheriff. "You're sure, Slade?

"Yes, I'm sure," El Halcon answered. He contemplated the dead outlaw a moment.

"They were smart, all right," he commented. "They figured out just what I'd be likely to do, ride up there alone. If it hadn't been for the slip the devil made, saying that he rode a mule down the canyon, they might have gotten away with it, for the trap was cleverly set. But when I couldn't find any mule tracks leading down the canyon, I got a mite suspicious, especially as I'd already decided that four horses went up the canyon instead of three, as he said."

"Yep, smart, but not quite smart enough to go up against a—against El Halcon," said the sheriff.

Grumley chuckled, not noticing the sheriff's slight slip. "El Halcon," he repeated. "That means The Hawk in Mexican lingo, don't it? Well, everybody knows that hawks are death on snakes. Here comes some folks to look over the carcasses; let's see what they have to say."

The visitors had plenty to say, but little of value. One or two bartenders were pretty sure they'd served one or more of the outlaws when they were alive, but were vague as to in whose company they might have been.

Which, Slade had to concede, was not surprising. With so many characters passing in and out of the town, it was hardly to be expected that saloon owners or workers would take any particular notice of an individual unless he did something to call attention to himself.

After the crowd of the morbid and curious had dispersed, Sheriff Harding Grumley and Slade repaired to the Square Deal for dinner. While they were eating, Dave Lang, the owner, came in. He was immaculately dressed, as usual, but walked with a slight limp as he approached the table.

"Congratulations," he said. "I just heard about it. I'd have been here sooner but my horse put his foot in a badger hole and fell and pitched me. Bruised my right hip pretty badly and I had to doctor it up a bit before heading for town. Harding, there ought to be a law against badger holes. Don't you think so, Slade?"

"They're treacherous things," Slade agreed.

"You did a bang-up job, Slade," Lang continued, his eyes, the hard glitter in them more pronounced than usual, roving over the room. "Yes, you're to be congratulated on your success against the lawless element. We need more of your kind here. As you all know, Amado Fuentes is my opponent in the race for mayor, but just the same I'd have hated to see anything like that happen to him. Some of his associates may be questionable characters, but I've never heard of him personally being mixed up in anything off-color. Well, have one on the house." He beckoned to a waiter, crossed to the bar, limping slightly, and after a moment of conversation with his head bartender, passed through a door that led to a back room.

"A nice feller," observed Sheriff Harding, sipping his drink. "I've a notion he'll make a good mayor, if he gets elected."

"If he gets elected," Slade repeated, and raised his own glass.

A few minutes later Dave Lang reappeared from the back room, carrying a large valise. He came straight to the table.

"Be seeing you gents in about a month," he said. "I've just got time to catch the ten-fifteen for San Francisco. Plan to study their system of city government. *Adios!*"

There was a derisive gleam in his glittering eyes as he nodded to Slade and the sheriff and walked away. Slade watched his tall form pass through the swinging doors.

"Well, I'll be hanged!" he murmured.

SEVENTEEN

SHERIFF HARDING contemplated his glass. "Dave's always doing things like that," he remarked. "Flies off somewhere with hardly a moment's notice, and sometimes doesn't show up again for weeks. I gather, though, that he's got wide interests over the state and even back east. Be a big man some day, I predict. He's got all the earmarks."

"Yes, all that's needed, rightly applied, to make him a success in any field of endeavor," Slade agreed soberly.

Sheriff Harding set down his empty glass. "Well, I feel in the need of a mite of rest," he said. "Better get it before Murrieta and his hellions bust loose someplace else."

"I don't think you will be bothered with Murrieta's activities for a while," Slade observed.

"You mean we've thinned out his bunch till he'll have to call a halt for a while?"

"In a way, yes," Slade answered. "I've a notion he's decided the section is a mite hot for him right now and will react accordingly."

"Don't exactly get what you mean, but the chances are you're right, whatever it is," conceded the sheriff. "Well, I'm going to bed."

Slade was right in his prediction. The days that followed were peaceful for Los Angeles. There were a few friendly stabbings in the Mexican quarter. Gamblers in the Alhambra disagreed and talked it over through the smoke. Some patrons of the Square Deal staged a corpse and cartridge session that resulted in punctured hides but no fatalities. Things the town marshal could handle by himself and which the sheriff's office did not deign to notice. After a week had passed, Slade dropped in on Sheriff Harding.

"Looks like you had the right slant and the hellion has pulled out," commented the sheriff. "Looks like he's gone for good."

116

"I imagine he plans to return eventually," Slade said.

"Now you've spoiled my whole day!" grumbled Harding.

"If you'll do what I ask, perhaps I can unspoil it for you," Slade smiled.

"I'll do anything I can," the sheriff promised. "What do you want me to do?"

"You can get in touch with the sheriff of Sacramento County?" Slade asked. Harding nodded.

"I'd like for you to get in touch with him," Slade continued. "Find out from him if there has been a noticeable increase in killing and robbing in his bailiwick and the neighboring counties. Especially where miners, prospectors and gold shipments are concerned."

Sheriff Harding stared. "You mean you figure the devil is operating up there in the Valley?"

"Get in touch with the sheriff," Slade suggested.

Hading did so, by telegraph. It didn't take long for him to get an answer.

"I've a notion if they'd sent it the way Tom Bullitt told it to them, it would have burnt up the wires," he chuckled. "Son, you hit the nail square on the head. There is a bunch operating up there, just like the Murrieta bunch operated here. Robbing and murdering miners and prospectors and cattle buyers. Stuck up a stage from Placerville and got away with a big gold shipment. Don't leave any witnesses, but it seems one jigger got a look at them and lived to tell about it. He said the hellion who 'peared to be running things is big and tall with black hair worn sort of long."

"The fellow I got a glimpse of there in that clearing and down the canyon trail was big and tall, but I didn't notice his hair," Slade said. "Yes, it's Murrieta, as he is called, and his sidewinders, the few he's got left."

"Bullitt mentioned that it 'pears to be a small band, not more than five or six," nodded the sheriff. "Here's his telegram—long as a letter."

Slade read the message carefully. However it contained nothing of significance the sheriff had not already mentioned. He passed it back to the peace officer and sat silent for some moments.

"Yes, it's the Murrieta bunch, all right," he repeated. "And it's what's left of the bunch, including the devil who is the leader, that I trailed from Texas."

"You feel sure of that?"

"I do."

"Then," said the sheriff, "I suppose you're going to hit the trail?"

"I am," Slade answered.

"You'll have no official authority up there," Harding reminded him.

"I think I'll be packing all I need," Slade replied.

Sheriff Harding glanced at the black butts of the big Colts flaring out from his sinewy hips and was inclined to agree.

"You're still a deputy sheriff of Los Angeles County," he observed. "I'll give you a leave of absence. That will give you a certain amount of official standing. If you get in trouble with the authorities up there, get word to me and I'll see what I can do. I know Tom Bullitt, the sheriff, well. If you happen to contact him in any way, mention my name."

"I'll do that, and thank you," Slade said. "Yes, I'm heading for Sacramento City."

"Taking the train?"

"If you can arrange for transportation for my horse. Otherwise, I'll ride."

"I can take care of that," promised Harding. "At midnight there's a combination passenger and stock train leaving here—the road has a regular run of that sort. I'll have your cayuse put in a car next to the caboose. It's done every now and then by cowmen down here who want to take along their pet saddle critters."

"That will be fine," Slade replied gratefully.

"Well, it's your picnic," said the sheriff. "I once said it was your funeral, but I've sort of changed my mind about that. I've a notion you'll come back, all right, and Murrieta won't."

"Hope you're right on both angles," Slade smiled.

EIGHTEEN

THE HOURS AFTER MIDNIGHT found Walt Slade comfortably ensconced in one of the three coaches attached to the stock train and headed north. On his left was the Coast Range, to the right the towering bulk of the Sierras. The train was primarily a stock train and wasted no time. Slade learned from the conductor that there would be a stop at a water tank about a dozen miles south of Sacramento City; he resolved to disembark there and continue the trip via horseback, reasoning he would attract less attention that way. Sheriff Harding had said a few words to the train crew, so Slade did not lack cooperation when it came to unloading Shadow. Sitting the tall black horse, he watched the train roar away into the north, then set out at a comfortable pace on the last leg of his journey.

He entered the Crescent City from the woods near the foot of P Street, found a stable for Shadow, enjoyed a good wash and put away a hearty meal at a busy restaurant. Eating slowly, he had a drink and smoked a couple of cigarettes. He had a feeling that the climax of the long and arduous chase was drawing near.

Full night had fallen when he left the restaurant and passed down J Street into a scene of roistering pandemonium equal to Los Angeles' "Alley" at its wildest. In every block a gambling house was going full blast, and numerous saloons. There was a din and clatter of music, a clinking of great piles of twenty-dollar gold pieces, a thudding of bags of gold-dust as the reckless miners threw them on the table to "go their pile" on the "eagle-bird" or bet a hundred ounces on the turn of a card. The air quivered to the constant cry of the roulette men: "Make the game, gents!" "Away she spins!" "Double O, red!" "Round she goes and round she goes! Where she stops nobody knows, except the devil, and he won't tell!"

119

The street was crowded with men of all colors and classes, on foot or on horseback, and with pack mules coming from or going to the mines. Slade had to shoulder his way through the sweating, booming, brawling throng.

He entered the great Humboldt gambling hall, famous all over California for years. It was literally swarming with gamblers and miners and hard-eyed watchful men. There were women, too, painted and powdered and gaudily dressed. At the bar Slade engaged a friendly bartender in conversation and soon had a pretty good line-up on the town's various places of entertainment.

"If you're really looking for excitement, cowboy, work on down J Street toward the river," the barkeep advised. "Here, with white chips a hundred dollars, there's too much money involved for cutting up to be allowed. But farther down the street, gentlemen, hush! They get saltier all the time. Down by the levee is the Empire; there the owl really hoots."

Leaving the Humboldt, Slade worked his way down J Street, visiting various saloons and gambling halls, drinking sparingly and watching the crowds. Realizing a growing weariness, the result of the long jolting train trip and the ride under a hot sun, he was about ready to call it a night when he reached the Empire saloon, restaurant and gambling hall of which the bartender spoke. He hesitated a moment, then decided to give the place a once-over before turning in.

The Empire was located close to the levee, near the foot of J Street, where the steamboats were tied up and the air quivered to the rumble of hand trucks, the creaking of winches and the shouts of stevedores. It was a rough and boisterous section into which the big saloon and gambling hall fitted nicely.

The Empire was big as the Humboldt, and as crowded. But here was a wilder note, a feeling of tenseness, a more turbulent gathering. More in evidence than at the Humboldt were men whose apparel proclaimed them as being fresh from the hills and the deserts. Here, too, was more than a sprinkling of individuals who, Slade decided, were neither professional gamblers, honest miners in town for a bust, nor cowhands celebrating after driving their herds to the mining communities. They were as hard a looking

bunch as any he had encountered in Los Angeles or else-
where.

As he stood watching, Slade's attention was gradually
drawn to a conversation in progress between two old
miners standing next to him at the bar. At first he listened
idly, then his interest quickened.

"Yes, those devils did it again," the elder of the two
suddenly remarked to his companion. "Three miners
headed for town with their clean-up, drygulched and
robbed of their pokes between Sutter's Fort and Placerville just about dark yesterday. I heard those three fellers
had hit a big pocket and were bringing in between thirty-
and forty-thousand dollars worth of gold. Not that it did
them any good. The blasted owlhoots got it all and all the
poor miners got was lead pizening."

"Figure they headed for town?" asked the other.

"Oh, sure," replied the first speaker. "They'd come here
for a bust and to change the gold into hard money.
Wouldn't be surprised if they're in this place right now.
Here they can change the dust for money and no questions asked. Always somebody bringing in gold to change,
and the Empire don't give a darn where they got it just
so long as they pay the premium for having it cashed. Yep,
I guarantee they headed for Sacramento. After they've had
a night or two in town, they'll slide back to Placerville,
the chances are. Up around there is where most of the
gold is coming from nowadays. And the devils always seem
to find out when somebody makes a big strike. It's a
blasted shame and the law officers don't seem able to do
anything about it. Never was such a bunch operating in
this section as has been for the past couple of weeks.
Smart as a treeful of owls and plumb deadly. Shoot first
and rob afterward. Nobody knows who they are, and
everybody's getting suspicious of everybody else."

The two miners finished their drinks and moved away.
Slade returned his attention to the crowd. Listening to the
miners' conversation, his weariness had fallen from him
like a cloak. He had anticipated a tedious sojourn in the
Crescent City and its environs while he tried to pick up
a clue that might lead him to the men he sought. Now
it looked like there was a good possibility that the hellions
might come to him. He ordered another drink.

Midnight came and went, and abruptly Slade's interest

was attracted to a man who had just walked in. A tall man with black hair grown rather long, his broad-brimmed black hat pulled low over his eyes. His face, dark almost as an Indian's, of which Slade caught but a fleeting glimpse, seemed vaguely familiar.

The man walked purposefully, weaving in and out of the crowd, as if he knew exactly where he was going. Slade left the bar and sauntered after him.

Getting through the press of the crowd, the man walked briskly to a door in the side wall of the room. He opened it and passed through, leaving it slightly ajar. Slade quickened his pace. He reached the door, opened it and stepped out into what appeared to be a dark alley—and looked squarely into the muzzle of a gun.

With a frantic twist he slewed sideways. The gun blazed and the tall figure of El Halcon reeled back, clutched at the wall for support and sank to the ground in a huddled heap. A tattoo of fast steps sounded down the alley, quickly fading into the distance.

Slade never did completely lose consciousness, but the terrific blow of the bullet that creased his head just above the left temple paraylzed his body to such an extent that it was some minutes before he could sit up, holding his throbbing head in his hands. For another minute or two he sat trying to rearrange his disordered faculties. Then he fumbled a handkerchief from his pocket and with a shaking hand swabbed away the blood that trickled down the side of his face.

"Outfoxed!" he muttered disgustedly. "The hellion spotted me as quickly as I spotted him, and recognized me. Knew exactly what to do, and did it! And I walked into the trap like a dumb yearling. Pure luck, nothing more, that he didn't drill me dead center."

After a while he stood up and leaned against the wall of the building till his head stopped whirling and the bell notes ceased to sound in his ears. He had closed the door behind him when he stepped out and apparently the shot had not been heard above the uproar inside, or had attracted no attention. He started to re-enter the saloon but changed his mind and walked to the end of the alley, which opened onto a lighted street. Rounding the block, he paused in front of the Empire, decided he'd had enough excitement for one day and, thoroughly disgusted, obtained a room in a small hotel nearby and went to bed. Almost instantly he was asleep.

Slade ate his breakfast in a little sidewalk restaurant and then sat smoking and debating his next move. He thought it very probable that Murrieta and his bunch had left town without delay. The question was, where would they go? Recalling the conversation between the two miners, he concluded that their most likely destination was Placerville or its environs. Mid morning found him riding across the valley to Placerville, some forty miles distant.

That night, Slade made camp on the bank of a little stream. Staple provisions he carried in his saddle pouches took care of all the needs of the inner man, while Shadow made out very well on grass. Getting an early start the next morning, he arived at Placerville shortly before noon.

Although tame compared to what it was in the boom days years before, when it was known as Hangtown and lived up to its name, Placerville was still plenty lively. The surrounding hills and deserts continued to produce large quantities of gold and the miners came Placerville to renew their supplies and enjoy a little diversion before returning to their claims. Sacramento was the goal when a big bust was in order, but Placerville served as a sort of stopgap between real celebrations. Which meant that there were always characters hanging around who preyed on the honest gold-seekers whenever opportunity provided.

After securing quarters for his horse and himself, and something to eat, Slade browsed around the town. During the afternoon, the shops and general stores were busy, but after darkness fell the saloons and gambling halls took over and Placerville began to howl. The saloons were filled with bearded and booted men of all nations and colors. Gold and nuggets heaped the tables, the sawdust-covered floors reeked with spilled whiskey and occasionally the raw and piercing smell of spilled blood.

Slade drifted from place to place, listening, observing. He soon learned that the most recent outrage of the owl-hoot band was a foremost topic of discussion and there was much conjecture as to the identity of the desperados. The general concensus of opinion appeared to be that they had come down from Nevada.

Not all the men crowding the saloons wore miners' garb, and there were hands that showed no marks of picks or shovel. These individuals, Slade noted, did more listening than talking.

As the night wore on, the red-eye the miners had consumed began getting in its licks. They grew talkative, loud and boastful, bragging about the rich strikes they had made and upholding their particular localities against all others. To these, Slade noticed, the quiet individuals who drank sparingly gave particular attention.

One stocky, big-featured miner standing near Slade had a deep and powerful voice that rose above all others.

"I tell you Skeleton Gulch is the up and coming diggin's," he declared to all and sundry. "There ain't no place in this section to equal the Gulch. Sure it's hard to get to and one devil of a hole to work but, gents, she pays off, she pays off! Me and my pardner have hit it rich there. I come in to get some mules from a feller I know. In the morning I'm heading back to the Gulch, where my pardner is waiting for me. Day after tomorrow we'll be back with our dust. Then we aim to make tracks for Sacramento and have us a time of times. Reckon we could just about buy that dang town with what we'll have in our pokes. Yes, sir, Skeleton Gulch is the real thing!"

The bartender who served Slade leaned close. "That feller's a plain darn fool," he said in low tones. "Braggin' that way about his strike and the dust he's going to be packin' in. Plenty of listening ears in this place. Strangers here tonight I ain't never seen before, and I don't care if I ever see 'em again, from the looks of them. That feller is just asking to have his brains blowed out and his dust lifted while he's packin' it to town. Mark my words on it, feller. You're a right lookin' hombre or I wouldn't be telling you this. Mark my words on it."

"Where is that place he's talking about? Is it really good ground?" Slade asked casually.

"Skelton Gulch? Yes, from what everybody says, I reckon there's good ground there, but it's one devil of a hole and hard to get to. The trail there runs through some mightly rough country and it really ain't much more than a game track. To get there you'd keep right up this street you're on now; it turns into a trail, the trail that leads to the main prospecting ground up to the northeast.

Ten miles out from here the trail forks and the right-hand fork, that darn snake track, runs almost due east. That's the trail to Skelton Gulch.

"Yep, I guess it's good ground there, as that loco loud-mouth keeps saying, but there's no grub and mighty little water, and what little there is is bad. Everything has to be packed in from down here and you have to know your business if you aim to stay alive. That's why more folks ain't heading that way. You have to be a desert and moun-tain man to get by in the Gulch. Well, there goes blabber-mouth out the door. Nobody following him—he ain't packing anything but a slim poke right now—but plenty got their eyes on him. Yes, sir, he's looking for trouble."

Slade thought so, too.

Shortly afterward, Slade retired to his room in the little hotel. Drawing a chair to an open window which overlooked the street, he sat down, rolled a cigarette and surveyed the changeful scene below, which in the dim light looked fantastic and unreal.

He pondered the colorful history of this gold strike town, with which he was fairly familiar.

Placerville was the site of the second real gold strike on the great "Mother Lode." The first had been at Coloma, nine miles to the north by slightly west, at a spot on the river the Indians called Culloomah, the site of the saw-mill operated by John Augustus Sutter. Jim Marshall, who worked for Sutter, while shutting off the water, hap-pened to notice flakes of gold. Marshall's discovery started the greatest and most romantic gold rush of all time.

Latecomers found the land around Coloma pretty well staked out, so they moved south and east. There two ranchers from the Sacramento Valley, Daylor and Mc-Coon, struck it rich at a point called "Old Dry Diggin's". They took $17,000 worth of gold from one small ravine in a week's time. Immediately there was a new rush with men swarming up and down the gulches around what first became known as Ravine City; soon afterward, Placerville.

But the miners were not the only ones to be drawn by the lure of easy wealth. Outlaws also poured in, many of them members of the notorious Owls who for a while terrorized San Francisco until they were driven out by vigilantes. The owlhoots thrived on easy pickings, for a while.

But the miners of Placerville were stern men. They declared war on the outlaws. One night three of the plundering band swooped down on a miner's cabin, beat the unfortunate man unmercifully and under gunpoint ransacked his cabin and stole fifty ounces of gold dust.

However, they didn't get a chance to enjoy the proceeds of their raid. The bruised and battered miner was able to give a good description of the devils and they were quickly captured.

The newly elected mayor of Placerville held court under a great oak tree that stood at the corner of Main and Coloma Streets. The three culprits were quickly tried and convicted. The mayor cocked an eye at a stout branch over his head.

"Reckon that one is strong enough to hold all three," he observed.

The three outlaws were hanged to the branch of the tree that was henceforth known as the hang tree. From that day on it was a busy tree indeed. The mayor thought that under its grateful shade was as good a place to hold court as any and proceeded to do so. The street became the mayor's courtroom and the crowd the jury for desperados brought before the court. No time was wasted and so many were hanged that Placerville soon became known, unofficially, as Hangtown. Slade chuckled as he recalled the fact. Just one thing wrong with the town based on what he had seen of it, he ruminated: They hadn't hanged enough.

From the very first Placerville was a strategic point on the overland trail and the Coloma Road. Through it passed the Overland Mail, the Pony Express and, later, the overland telegraph. When the rush to the Comstock Lode in Nevada began, Placerville became the chief station on the way from the west. Through it poured a stream of ponderous wagons drawn by six-mule teams, bearing merchandise and provisions to the Washoe mines. Placerville boomed and soon became a serious contender with San Francisco and Sacramento in wealth and population. During those wild days, men who were later to become industrial giants began their careers there; such men as Mark Hopkins, the railroad magnate, Philip D. Armour, the meat-packing tycoon, and John Studebaker, who got his start building miners' wheelbarrows.

For a while Placerville bade fair to become California's leading city; but a gold strike is seldom something upon which permanency is built. Now Placerville was just another mining town, chiefly dependent on supplies sold miners from the surrounding hills and the gold they brought in for a bust.

But the town was still plenty turbulent and prosperous, Slade was willing to admit, and there were still pickings for the owlhoots. It was ideal headquarters for such a gang as the Murrieta bunch, where they could pick up information and plan their raids on defenseless miners who had struck it rich and were bringing their gold to town.

The history of Placerville was a history of violence, crime and sudden wealth. And such a history long remains a lodestone for the unscrupulous.

He hoped the bunch would believe that the bullet which struck him down outside the Empire saloon had killed or incapacitated him. If such were the case, they would be relieved of worry so far as he was concerned and would feel freer to operate.

He went to bed and was up again with the first light. Before the dawn fully broke he rode out of town, following the well-travelled trail that ran northeast.

The loquacious bartender was a good estimator of distance. Just about ten miles from Placerville the trail forked, the main road continuing northeast, the fork turning due east. It was a dim and rocky track that slithered over low hills, through deep hollows and between thickets of chaparral and clumps of chimney rock. To the south was rolling brush country, while on the north the track was flanked by a fairly steep slope likewise covered with growth.

Slade rode for several miles. In a dense thicket which overlooked the trail he tethered Shadow and concealed himself in the fringe of the brush.

A couple of hours passed and he heard a plodding of hoofs on the rocks from the same direction in which he had come. A little later a man hove into view, riding one mule and leading two others loaded with supplies. Slade recognized the talkative miner of the night before.

The miner's eyes were slightly bleary from his overnight potations but he whistled cheerily as he rode past, shoulders squared, one work-hardened hand affectionately caressing the neck of the mule. He'd had his bust and felt fine.

Slade smiled as he watched him fade into the distance. The sort that would settle down after a while, rear a family and become a pillar of the community. That is, if he got the chance to live that long. Slade's eyes turned cold again and his face was bleak as he surveyed the forbidding terrain ahead. The section was ideal for outlaw depredations.

Adapting his pace to that of the mules ahead, he followed the trail while the sun climbed the long ladder of the sky, crossed the zenith and slanted westward. All the while he appeared to be steering for a range of tall hills which raked the eastern horizon with broken-nailed fingers of stone.

The sun was low in the west when he saw a raw, red gash in the hills ahead. Into this ominous gorge the trail vanished. This, Slade presumed, was Skeleton Gulch; from its looks, it doubtless did not belie its sinister name. He did not enter the Gulch but made his camp in a thicket off the trail and some distance from the dark gap.

The first streak of dawn found him awake. Long before the early sunlight flowed like water over the crest of the eastern hills, he had cooked and eaten his breakfast of bread, bacon and steaming coffee. Lounging in the shadow of the growth, he watched the gulch mouth until he saw two men mounted on mules and leading a loaded third ride from the gap.

Soon he recognized one as the miner he had trailed the day before. The other was older and of lanky build. They were chattering gaily, with frequent laughter, as they rode past his place of concealment, apparently not in the least apprehensive of danger. Slade reflected how easy it would be for him to kill both and make off with the led mule. The aparejo or pack sack on the animal's back was well plumped out and the mule walked as if it were heavy. It was logical to assume the sack contained the miners' dust and nuggets. If so, they had struck it rich.

He waited until the pair had passed his hiding place and gotten some distance ahead. Then he sent Shadow through the chaparral which flanked the trail, high up enough so he could keep an eye on the winding track a considerable distance to the front of the plodding mules. The going was rough, but Shadow was used to such work and made no slips.

All day long Slade rode, never losing sight of the pair, eyes constantly searching the terrain ahead.

The sun dropped down the sky until its lower edge was touching the crests of the western hills far across the great Sacramento Valley. The miners were pushing the mules now, evidently anxious to reach the forks and the main Placerville trail before dark.

Slade quickened Shadow's pace until he was directly opposite the hurrying pair and no great distance above them. If the attempt were to be made at all, it would be made quickly. The main trail now only a few miles ahead was open, heavily travelled and not favorable to ambush.

The mules were toiling up a sag. From his greater elevation, Slade could see over the crest of the rise sooner than could the miners on the trail. As his gaze cleared the level of the crest, four men rode out of the chaparral flanking the farther slope and urged their horses swiftly upward to meet the oncoming miners. As they did so, they drew rifles from their saddle boots. Slade unsheathed his heavy Winchester and cocked it.

Just below the lip of the rise, the four horsemen halted, rifles at the ready. The far slope of the sag was much steeper than that which the miners were ascending; the drygulchers would see them before they were themselves sighted. Also, the blinding rays of the setting sun would dazzle the eyes of their intended victims, while the outlaws would have the sun at their backs.

Slade sent Shadow surging forward to where a small open clearing, less than a hundred yards from where the outlaws sat their horses, freed him of the intervening brush that might spoil his aim. He reached it as the miners topped the slope and started across the short level of the crest. The drygulchers raised their rifles. Slade jerked Shadow to a sliding halt, clamped the Winchester to his shoulder.

The rifle wisped smoke. The report slammed back and forth between the rocks, One of the outlaws whirled from his saddle like a wind-blown leaf. The others writhed about, saw the horseman outlined against the background of the growth and opened fire at him.

Slade felt bullets fan his face, rip the sleeve of his shirt. He fired as fast as he could work the ejection lever, again and again.

A second drygulcher spun from the saddle; the Winchester cracked a report and a third man went down. The remaining outlaw, broad of shoulder, black of hair, was working the ejection lever of his rifle frantically to free a jammed mechanism.

Slade's voice rang out.

"Trail's end, Lang! Give up!"

Dave Lang didn't give up. He clanged the lever shut, flung the rifle to his shoulder. Slade pulled trigger—and the hammer clicked on an empty shell!

Lang's rifle spurted reddish fire. The tall form of El Halcon slewed sideways in the saddle and fell to the ground to lie motionless. Lang whirled his horse, sent him charging into the sea of brush and vanished from sight.

NINETEEN

SLADE LAY with his slitted eyes fixed on the spot where Lang had disappeared. Satisfied that the outlaw had kept going, he rose to his feet, called reassuringly to the frightened miners and stuffed fresh cartridges into the magazine of his rifle. With the Winchester at the ready, he walked to where the three drygulchers lay. All three were dead. Slade walked back to Shadow.

"I believe I fooled him," he told the horse. "If I didn't, he'll very likely pull out of the country and the chances are we'll never come up with him. If I did, I figure he'll head for Sacramento and Los Angeles, believing that he finished me and hasn't anything to worry about. Well, time that grinds the rocks will tell us all."

Sliding the Winchester into the boot, he mounted and rode slowly down the slope. The miners showed signs of beating a retreat, but Slade called to them that everything was under control and they had nothing more to fear. They stared at him with scared faces but stood their ground as he pulled Shadow to a halt and dismounted.

"Some devils must have spotted you from the top of that tall hill over to the west, just this side of the main trail," he told them. "They evidently figured you were packing dust and decided this sag would be a proper place to lay for you. I was riding up there on the slope and saw what they were up to, just in time."

The miners were too excited and grateful to wonder how he happened to be riding the slope instead of the trail at such an opportune time, and Slade did not see fit to enlighten them. They were profuse in their thanks and told him their names were Lije Bixby and Gus Flint. Slade supplied his own name and they shook hands with vigor.

"Think it's safe to go on to town, or had we better hole up here for the night?" Bixby, the elder, asked.

131

"Getting dark fast and there's no telling what we might run into, even on the main trail," Slade replied. "No sense in playing your luck too strong. I'd say let's slide up to that cleared space—I saw a trickle of water there—and make camp."

Slade had his own reason for not wanting to proceed to Placerville before morning. He could hardly escape being noticed and the word that he was still alive might reach Lang's ears and then the hellion might well pull out for good. For the same reason he preferred for the miners not to get a chance to spread the story of their escape from the drygulchers before the following day.

Bixby and Flint didn't argue the point and busied themselves making camp. They had plenty of provisions in their pouches and Flint soon threw together an appetizing meal.

As they ate, the two miners' heads drew together and they talked for a moment in low tones. They drew apart and Bixby wiped his bearded lips with the back of a horny hand.

"Slade," he said, "in that packsack over there is a heap of gold. Took us a long time to wash it out, and it was a hard chore. If It hadn't been for you, those hellions would be packing it away right now, and Gus and me would be layin' down there in the trail. So we've 'greed that a hefty portion of it should go to you for what you did for us."

Slade smilingly shook his head. "It was a real pleasure to help worth-while folks," he said. "I wouldn't take pay for it. Thanks, very much, oldtimers. Just having the privilege to lend you a hand was pay enough. Now I vote we clean up and knock off a mite of shut-eye. I didn't get much last night."

"Me, either," chuckled Flint. "Yep, let's hit the hay."

In the dark hour before the dawn, Slade arose and quietly got the rig on Shadow. He led the black horse to the trail, mounted and rode west. He did not wish to enter Placerville in company with the miners, knowing that they would quickly talk of what happened. He bypassed the town and headed for Sacramento.

When Bixy and Flint awoke, they were greatly astonished to find their benefactor had disappeared.

"Where did he come from and where did he go?"

wondered Flint. "All of a sudden he just happened, and now all of a sudden he just ain't."

Old Lije Bixby, a deeply religious man, was thoroughly grounded in the Scriptures. Now he quoted a verse that he felt fitted the case precisely.

"Be not forgetful to entertain strangers: for thereby some have entertained angels unawares."

Slade was in a grimly complacent mood as he rode across the valley. One by one, directly or indirectly, he had accounted for the Murrieta band, the murderers of the Texas cowhands in the valley east of El Paso. The score was more than evened up, so far as numbers were concerned, for undoubtedly only a part of the outfit had ridden on the foray into Texas. All, that is, except the vicious leader. With Dave Lang killed or in jail awaiting execution for California murders, the tally would be complete.

"I'm pretty sure the devil will stop for maybe a day or two in Sacramento," he told Shadow. "Figuring me out of the way, he'll be in no hurry. He may even have another little chore or two lined up. His bunch is done for, but he wouldn't have any trouble rounding up a few hellions to lend a hand if he has something in mind. I gathered from what Sheriff Harding said that he's been up this way before and is familiar with the lay of the land and conditions here. I'm banking on him hanging around that Empire saloon if he does stay in town for a while. That's where we'll look for him, and if we find him we'll settle this business one way or the other for good and all. June along, horse, we should make it across the valley by dark; you can take it. Extra helping of oats for you when you get to Sacramento; I'm staying empty right along with you."

Slade estimated correctly. The lovely blue dusk was sitting over the valley like impalpable dust and the western sky was a marvel of flaming color as he rode through the outskirts of the Crescent City. He stabled his horse, made sure that all its wants were provided for, then repaired to a nearby restaurant and ordered everything in sight. Although quite tired, he made a round of the J Street saloons and gambling houses, saw nothing of interest and went to bed.

The next two nights were a repetition of the first, and

Slade began to wonder if he mightn't be wrong in figuring that Dave Lang would pause in Sacramento before heading for Los Angeles.

There was also the disquieting possibility that Lang, not certain that his enemy suffered a mortal wound, had decided to take no chances and had pulled out for parts unknown. If so, he could have gone in any direction. Down the river by boat, into the hills, across the Sierras to Nevada. And wherever he turned up there would be more robberies, more killing of innocent people. Slade experienced a growing uneasiness as he made the rounds for the fourth time without sighting his quarry.

Slade lingered over his breakfast the following morning. For a long time he sat sipping coffee, smoking and thinking. His lack of success in his quest depressed and annoyed him.

The paramount question was, had Lang paused at Sacramento or had he kept moving, headed for some destination unknown?

He tried to put himself in the place of the outlaw, to react as he would be expected to react under the circumstances. If Lang believed he had slain the man who had so persistently dogged his trail, would he not crave a period of relaxation, a chance to take it easy for a spell and recuperate from the strain of nervous tension under which he must have labored for so long? And Sacramento was the ideal spot for him to do so.

On the other hand, if he was not sure his enemy was dead, he would very likely hole up for a while, keeping under cover until his pursuer would grow discouraged or come to the conclusion that he was on the wrong track.

As a result of his ruminations he started work on a new tack, a systematic round of hotels and rooming houses, giving particular attention to those in the neighborhood of J Street and the waterfront. He questioned desk clerks and superintendents, giving a detailed description of the man he sought, evaluating the answers he received, alert for some chance remark that might prove significant. With negative results. Everybody appeared willing to cooperate, but nobody, it seemed, was able to recall contacting a man who answered to Dave Lang's description.

Finally, weary and footsore from endless tramping, he sat down on a bench in a little park, rolled a cigarette and again gave himself over to exhaustive thought. Of course, Sacramento was a big town and he could not hope to cover all of it in a short period of time. Also, Lang might have friends in the city who would shelter him and keep him out of sight. That also must be taken into account.

Then, after his second cigarette, he had an inspiration. Pinching out the butt, he left the park and began a round of livery stables. Once again he had no luck until dark was falling. From the garrulous old keeper of a small "horse hotel" not far from J Street, he got something that looked like pay dirt.

"Big tall feller, sort of broad, with black hair sort of long, and funny looking eyes," ruminated the keeper. "No, I ain't keeping a horse for a feller like that, but I'll tell you something. Just the other day I bought a horse from a feller who looks sort of like that. Uh-huh, that might be the feller. He came here to put up his cayuse. A fine looking critter, all right, and I said so. Feller said, 'Like to buy him?' I asked him how much he wanted for the plug, figuring what he'd say would be way beyond what I could pay. He named the price and it was mighty, mighty low for such a good-looking animal. Course I didn't jump in right away. I sort of hemmed and hawed and acted like I was doing him a favor. Don't think I fooled him much, 'cause he just sort of grinned. Thought of asking why he wanted to let the horse go for so little but figured that was his business, not mine. So I bought the cayuse, and figured I got a bargain. That's it over in the third stall."

Slade gave the horse a careful once-over. It was a dark chestnut and a fine animal. He had not given Dave Lang's mount much attention during the hectic encounter on the Placerville trail, but he seemed to recall that his horse was also a chestnut, at least dark in color. And the description the old keeper gave of the man from whom he had purchased the animal tallied quite well with Dave Lang's general appearance.

The keeper gave Slade a nervous glance and his voice was a bit apprehensive when he spoke.

"Think maybe that feller stole the horse, that was why he let go so cheap?" he asked.

Slade smiled and shook his head. "I don't think you need bother yourself on that score," he replied. "Highly unlikely that he stole it. Looks like you just got a nice

bargain, perhaps because he had no further use for the
horse at this time and was glad to get it off his hands."

"Well, I'm glad to hear you say that," the keeper said
in relieved tones. "You know, you sort of look like a
lawman, and I was getting scared."

"You don't need to be," Slade chuckled. "And thanks
very much for what you told me." He left the stable and
walked slowly to his room. Anyhow, it appeared that
Lang (he was quite confident that the horse seller was
Lang) did not contemplate making for the hills.

And Slade believed he was still in the city. After eating
and resting a while he again began making rounds of the
J Street saloons and gambling houses. In the Empire he
spotted his man. Wearing a long black coat, a ruffled
white shirt and a broad-brimmed black "J.B.", he was
near the middle of the room, talking to one of the dance
floor girls.

The recognition was instantly mutual. Lang's eyes
widened in incredulous disbelief, then his hand flashed
to his left armpit. There was a gleam of metal, the crash
of a shot.

Slade felt the wind of the passing bullet that smashed
the back-bar mirror to smithereens. He jerked his own gun
but was forced to hold his fire because the dance floor
girl was squarely between him and his opponent.

Lang whirled and streaked through the crowd, knock-
ing men right and left, overturning chairs and tables. Slade
went after him.

The room was in an uproar. Yells, curses, the crash
of broken furniture, the thud of falling men and the
screeches of women set the hanging lamps to dancing.
Slade did not dare shoot for fear of hitting someone in
the milling crowd. He holstered his gun. His own charging
passage through the throng added to the confusion. He
stumbled over men scrambling to their feet, caromed off
overturned tables, reeled and staggered as splintered chair
rungs rolled beneath his feet.

Lang reached the far side of the room, jerked open a
door and vanished through it. As Slade reached the
door he heard the fugitive's boots pounding up a stair.
He caught a glimpse of his coattails whisking around a
turn and raced in pursuit. Lang appeared thoroughly familiar with the ramifications of the building and apparently

knew just where he was going. But Slade was gaining on him.

Slade reached the stairhead, which opened onto a short hall. Lang was sliding through a door at the far end less than a dozen feet distant. Slade leaped after him, flung the sagging door wide in time to see Lang fall over a chair in the middle of a small room. His gun went clattering across the floor, but Lang leaped to his feet, flung open another door and bounded down a flight of stairs, Slade close on his heels.

He was almost within arm's length of the fugitive as Lang reached the bottom of the stairs, whisked through yet another door into what looked like a storeroom, in the far wall of which yawned a dark opening some seven feet in height and perhaps four in width. Lang dived into the opening, Slade after him.

A breath of dank air struck the Ranger's face. He heard a scurrying of tiny paws and a hurricane of squeals as huge river rats fled wildly. Ahead, a dozen feet or so was the other end of the timber-walled and roofed tunnel, which evidently opened onto the river. Lang bounded forward and had covered more than half the distance to the far opening when Slade's clutching hand closed on his shoulder. He whirled about, screaming a curse, and the Ranger found himself fighting for his life. A fist smashed against his jaw, a throttling hand grasped his throat.

Lang was a big man, tall almost as Slade, and pounds heavier. And his strength was the strength of a maniac. Slade seized his corded wrist and prevented the strangling fingers from getting a full grip, but break Lang's hold he could not. With his other hand he strove to fend off the blows Lang rained upon him. There was no chance to draw a gun, nothing to do but battle it out with bare hands.

Back and forth among the shrieking rats they lurched and reeled, slamming into the timbered walls of the tunnel, slipping, sliding on the wet stone flags. Slade was gasping for breath, the ever tightening grip of the madman on his throat was strangling the life out of him. Red flashes stormed before his eyes, bell notes rang in his ears. Down the tunnel they stumbled until they were almost at its outer brink, the river running swift and silent below.

A rat squealed its death agonies as Slade's boot crushed

it. His foot slipped on the pulpy carcass and he fell to one
knee. Lang roared in triumph.

With the strength of desperation, Slade lunged forward
and gripped the other about the thighs. He surged erect
and hurled Lang over his shoulder. Lang shrieked as he
flew through the air. His head struck the side timbers
with a crunching thud. He fell to the floor, his limbs
flopping grotesquely, and slid over the tunnel's outer lip.
From below drifted the sound of a sullen splash.

Breathing in great gasps, Slade stumbled to the tunnel
mouth and looked out. The surface of the river, silver
on black in the moonlight, was unbroken. But under the
dark water a flaccid, sodden thing that had been a man
hurried on a last long journey to the sea.

Slade leaned against the wooden wall, too spent to move.
He wondered idly what was the purpose of this passage
from the building to the river. Very probably to receive
cargoes of supplies brought from the river steamers. Feeling better but still rather shaky, he turned and retraced
his steps to the storeroom into which the tunnel emptied.
He could hear excited voices above. Stepping to the foot
of the stairs he glanced upward. Faces were peering down,
but nobody ventured to descend until the outraged and
empurpled dignity of the Empire's headwaiter shouldered
through the crowd and pounded down the steps.

"What is the meaning of this, sir?" he demanded.
"Scaring people out of their wits and breaking the furniture! Who was that man you were trying to kill? You had
better explain, sir, or I'll have the law on you."

Slade let his cold gaze rest on the face of the waiter,
who abruptly fell silent. Slipping his Ranger badge from
its pocket, he held it in front of the man's eyes, covering
the word "Texas" with his finger.

The waiter stared at the gleaming star and his voice became conciliatory.

"I'm sorry, sir," he said. "I didn't realize you were an
officer. Was the man you were pursuing dangerous?"

"If you'd gotten in his way you would have found out—
in the next world," Slade told him.

The waiter whitened visibly. "Where—where is he?"
he asked, glancing nervously about.

"He went into the river," Slade replied. The waiter
gasped.

"Is—is there anything I can do, sir?" he asked.

"Yes," Slade said. "Show me a way out of here so I won't have to pass through the crowd upstairs."

"Right this way, sir," said the waiter. He led the way to another door which opened onto an alley. "Right around the next corner and you'll reach J Street, sir," he said.

"Thank you," Slade nodded. "Good night."

"Good night, sir," the waiter replied in relieved tones, and slammed the door.

Slade circled J Street and reached his room. His face was bruised, his throat sore, and one eye was swelling. He smeared some ointment on his hurts and went to bed.

TWENTY

SLADE LEFT SACRAMENTO the following afternoon. He did not take a train, feeling that after the days of turmoil a leisurely ride down the state would be relaxing.

It proved to be so and he enjoyed every mile of it, surrounded as he was by the mighty scenery of the Golden State, its changeful panorama unfolding page by page under the blazing sun or by the light of the quiet stars. A region of story and legend, with a romantic past and a glamorous future. Slade experienced a sense of quiet satisfaction in having been instrumental, if only in a small way, toward bringing closer the days of peace and prosperity that would bless the land in years to come. He was in fine fettle when he at last reached the City of the Angels and gazed toward the sinister beauty of the Mohave Desert, across which ran the trail to home.

After caring for his horse he visited Sheriff Harding. The old peace officer listened in blank amazement at the tale he had to tell.

"Dave Lang!" he exclaimed, shaking his grizzled head when Slade paused. "Dave Lang! I'd never have believed it. He always seemed such a nice feller."

"A strange character," Slade said. "Shrewd, able, ambitious and far-seeing; but, I think, partly insane; his eyes always looked it. Capable of being successful in any line of endeavor, but the sort that would rather make a crooked dollar than an honest one. He could have very likely been elected mayor of a growing town and would have perhaps ended up governor of the state, to be written down in history as a statesman and an outstanding citizen. The old story of Esau over again—traded his birthright for a mess of pottage, and ended up spoiling the pottage before he got a chance to eat it."

"How'd you get a line on him?" asked the sheriff. "I

never saw anything about him I'd have called suspicious."

"What first got me to thinking about him was his hair," Slade replied.

"His hair?"

"That's right. Remember the night he signed the waiter's check, insisting that we have our food and drinks on the house? I was sitting opposite him and when he bent over to sign the check I got a good look at his hair. Down close to his scalp it was black."

"Black!"

"Yes; it showed plainly in the part. He neglected to touch up his bleaching job a mite too long."

"You mean he dyed his hair?" the sheriff asked incredulously.

"That's right," Slade nodded. "Bleached it yellow, rather. That set me to wondering about him. A woman may change the color of her hair sometimes for reasons of vanity, but not a man. He has to have a much more substantial reason for doing so. Why did Lang do it? Obviously, to change his appearance. And he did change it, greatly. Also, it was in the nature of a trade mark. His yellow hair, in contrast to his dark complexion, attracted people's attention to the exclusion of the rest of his appearance; they'd notice the hair and not much else about him. And why should he want to change his appearance? Again the answer was obvious: so he wouldn't be recognized by someone who had seen him before, presumably under radically different circumstances. I expect if you'd trace him back, you'd find he was wanted in quite a few places."

"And he allowed it to grow out black again after he left Los Angeles?"

Slade shook his head. "That would have taken much too long," he explained. "He used a simple dye on it the Indians employed in their ceremonials. I've used it myself a couple of times, when I wanted my skin the color of a Mexican's with a lot of Indian blood. Plain water doesn't affect it, but plenty of soap washes it out easily enough. He used some on his face, too, and the change in his appearance was remarkable. When I spotted him in the Empire saloon, I wasn't at all sure of him—his face just seemed vaguely familiar. Then he made one of the slips he'd been making ever since I showed up in the section—he tried to kill me in the alley back of the saloon. Then I knew he was my man."

"You showing up here and downing Slow Baker after doing for three of his bunch out on the desert must have given him something of a jolt," the sheriff observed reflectively.

"Yes, I think it did," Slade agreed. "Anyhow he began making slips. He made a bad one when he kidnapped Amado Fuentes. Why should anybody want to kill Fuentes? Who would profit by it? So far as I could learn the only person was Lang, who by so doing would eliminate Fuentes from the mayoralty race and insure the election of Lang, whose objective, of course, was to get his fingers in the municipal till. And when I heard him shout 'Let them have it!' up there in the clearing where Fuentes was held prisoner, I was sure it was the same voice that shouted the same words back in Texas. Which meant the speaker was the hellion I'd been trailing."

"Do you think Lang realized you were a Texas Ranger?" asked Harding.

"I don't think so, otherwise he might have reacted differently," Slade said. "I think he just figured me to be a smart owlhoot trying to horn in on his preserves after pulling the wool over your eyes. As it was, all he hankered for was a showdown with me personally and got careless."

Slade paused to roll and light a cigarette.

"His pulling out of the section was also significant. His bunch had been just about cleaned up, so he decided to take the few that remained and skalleyhoot to new fields for a while until things cooled down here. And again he slipped. After he left, I did a mite of investigating at the railroad station and learned he'd bought a ticket to Sacramento, not San Francisco as he had announced his intention of doing."

"You Rangers don't miss a bet!" the sheriff exclaimed admiringly.

"We are trained not to, and taught not to ignore the smallest detail, which may prove important," Slade smiled. "Well, I guess that's about all. Fuentes will be elected and I think he'll make a good mayor. You'll need one. This town is going to grow and it will keep on growing."

Slade was right in his prediction. The next two years

would see the population of Los Angeles more than quadrupled.

He stood up, smiling down at the old peace officer. "I'm heading back to Texas," he announced. "First, though, I want to send Captain McNelty a wire. He may have something lined up for me that I can handle on the way."

Slade sent the wire, which read:

> "It was finished in California. Any orders?
> I'm riding east."

Very quickly an answer came.

> "This time ride to the Atlantic, blast you!
> Then bridge *it* and keep going."

Slade chuckled as he went to get his horse. Undoubtedly Captain Jim was pleased.

THE END